DOUBLE FAULT 7

TYNDALE HOUSE PUBLISHERS, INC., CAROL STREAM, ILLINOIS

JERRY B. JENKINS · CHRIS FABRY

Thanks to Joey Johnson for his tennis expertise.

Visit Tyndale's exciting Web site for kids at www.tyndale.com/kids.

TYNDALE is a registered trademark of Tyndale House Publishers, Inc.

The Tyndale Kids logo is a trademark of Tyndale House Publishers, Inc.

Double Fault

Copyright © 2005 by Jerry B. Jenkins. All rights reserved.

Cover and interior photographs copyright © 2004 by Brian MacDonald. All rights reserved.

Cover photograph of tennis court © by Photos.com. All rights reserved.

Authors' photograph © 2004 by Brian MacDonald. All rights reserved.

Designed by Jacqueline L. Nuñez

Edited by Lorie Popp

Published in association with the literary agency of Alive Communications, Inc., 7680 Goddard Street, Suite 200, Colorado Springs, CO 80920.

Scripture quotations are taken from the *Holy Bible,* New Living Translation, copyright © 1996, 2004 by Tyndale House Foundation. Used by permission of Tyndale House Publishers, Inc., Carol Stream, Illinois 60188. All rights reserved.

This novel is a work of fiction. Names, characters, places, and incidents either are the product of the authors' imagination or are used fictitiously. Any resemblance to actual events, locales, organizations, or persons, living or dead, is entirely coincidental and beyond the intent of either the authors or publisher.

For manufacturing information regarding this product, please call 1-800-323-9400.

Library of Congress Cataloging-in-Publication Data

Jenkins, Jerry B.
  Double fault / Jerry B. Jenkins, Chris Fabry.
    p. cm. — (Tyndale kids) (Red Rock mysteries ; 7)
    Summary: After joining a tennis camp at a local country club, twins Ashley and Bryce Timberline are blamed for outbreaks of vandalism there, and must work not only to clear their names, but also to find the real culprit.
    ISBN 978-1-4143-0146-4 (pbk.)
    [1. Tennis—Fiction. 2. Christian life—Fiction. 3. Family life—Colorado—Fiction. 4. Colorado—Fiction. 5. Twins—Fiction. 6. Vandalism—Fiction. 7. Mystery and detective stories.] I. Fabry, Chris, date. II. Title. III. Series.
    PZ7.J4138Dou 2005
    [Fic]—dc22   2005010228

Printed in the United States of America

15 14
8   7   6   5   4

To Dave "Optical Illusion" Fabry

"Never discuss LOVE
with TENNIS PLAYERS; it means
NOTHING to them."

Anonymous

"The DEPRESSING thing
about TENNIS is that no matter how
GOOD I get, I'll never be as good as a WALL."

Mitch Hedberg

CHAPTER 1

✖ Ashley ✖

I heard Bryce through my headset. "Stay to the right. Car coming fast." He's my twin brother and thinks he has to watch out for me.

We were riding our ATVs on Top of the Crest, a narrow road that leads to the Red Rock Country Club. We hardly ever drive on regular roads, but Bryce and I had figured a way to get from our house to the country club through farmland and over Red Rock Mountain. In a car it takes 10 minutes—but 25 by ATV.

Before you think we're rich or something, you have to know that we don't belong to the country club. Too expensive. But it was a few weeks until our family vacation, and Bryce had spotted a tennis camp in the local paper. Our mom was happy to get us out of the house and have us stop moaning, "There's nothing to do."

The road had no yellow line and was barely wide enough for two small cars. Pine trees lined either side of the blacktop. My brother kept barking orders to me.

Finally I said, "Bryce, I know how to drive!"

Bryce followed me around a corner, where the mountains came into view. In the winter, Pikes Peak is all white, and the Front Range wears a furry coat. But now, in the middle of summer, the peak is brown and everything else is green. It gets so hot that forest fires can start with a lightning strike.

Wearing a helmet, you don't hear much but the wind, the ATV, and your heart, but I heard the car behind me.

"Ashley, look out!"

CHAPTER 2

☺ *Bryce* ☺

The silver car passed me in a blur, and I put on my brakes and yelled at Ashley. She swerved just in time to avoid it, but her right tire ran off the road. I thought she was going to flip, but she slammed on her brakes and skidded to within inches of a pine tree.

I pulled over and ran to her. She already had her helmet off.

"What was that guy thinking?" she said.

"You okay?"

"He didn't even slow down. Did you get a look at the car?"

"Corvette," I said. "Probably costs more than Sam makes in a year."

Sam is our stepdad. He met Mom at a memorial service for people who died in a plane crash, including our real dad. Sam's wife and younger daughter died on the same plane. We lived in Chicago then, but we moved to Colorado and Mom got remarried. That was before Mom became a Christian.

We have an older stepsister, Leigh, and a little brother, Dylan. Sam's a nice guy, and he has an interesting job—he flies a charter plane—but he doesn't believe the same as Mom and Ashley and me. We pray a lot for him and Leigh.

Ashley said, "All I saw was the driver's hair. He looked like some kind of model."

Just as we were about to get back on the road, another car pulled up. A woman got out and hurried over. She had short brown hair and wore khaki pants with a denim shirt. "You kids all right?" she said.

"My sister almost got run over."

The woman clucked her tongue. "That's all we need, a lawsuit against one of our employees." She held out a hand. "I'm Jill Davidson. I work at the club."

I told her our names.

Then Ashley said, "You know who that guy was?"

I described the car, and she glanced at our tennis rackets and bags strapped to our ATVs. "I think so, and my guess is you're going to meet him soon. You're headed to tennis camp, right?"

I nodded.

"Stop by my office after the morning session, and I'll give you a lunch voucher. That's the least we can do for you."

CHAPTER 3

❀ Ashley ❀

There's a reason Bryce wanted to enroll in the tennis camp. He's good. He can move around the court and get to just about any shot. I guess he's a natural. I have to work harder, but my dancing helps my coordination.

We parked on the upper tier of the parking lot, where men were preparing to play golf. Bryce pointed to the employee parking lot. The silver car sat in the shade—taking up two spaces.

Even before we reached the outdoor courts, I heard the *thwop* of tennis balls. There's nothing like the feel of a ball you hit right in the middle of the strings.

When we got to the courts, my heart sank. There were about 30 middle schoolers milling around in stylish tennis clothes. Bryce and I wore cutoff jeans and T-shirts. A few high schoolers were showing off, hitting overheads and laughing.

I recognized only a couple of kids from our school but felt better when I saw Hayley Henderson, one of my best friends.

"Seen the instructor yet?" she said as I sat next to her. "He looks like that marathon runner with the wavy hair and . . ."

Hayley prattled on about how cute this guy was, but I didn't care. I was studying her outfit, a nice white dress with a navy collar. "Was there some kind of dress code for this?" I said.

"You didn't read the brochure?" She put a hand on my arm and leaned close. "Don't worry. This place is in too much trouble to turn anybody away."

"Trouble?" I said.

"Haven't you heard?" She rubbed her fingers together. "Money problems. My dad told me all about it. They're losing cash every month with the upkeep of the golf course and salaries. It's why they're having these summer day camps—so they don't have to close."

It was hard to care about the club's money troubles when I was in a fashion nightmare. I've dreamed about being at school in my underwear, and this was about as bad.

"You and Bryce in the doubles track?" Hayley said.

I nodded.

"I'm sure you'll beat us." She giggled.

"Who are you playing with?"

She stood. "Duncan Swift."

There was a backhand to the heart. Hayley knew I'd had a crush on Duncan for years. I just sat there with my mouth open.

CHAPTER 4

☺ *Bryce* ☺

It's weird how you can spot a good tennis player without ever seeing him play. With basketball you could be eight feet tall, have arms like tree limbs, and be dorky with the ball. Or four-foot-three and able to dunk. But in tennis, if you're not thin and agile and don't walk with the confidence of a prizefighter, forget it. If you're plump, good players run you to death. If you don't have the strength to hit hard, opponents rush the net and smack your shots away like flies off a screen door.

I noticed a kid with a collared shirt and matching shorts. He had a little insignia over his shirt pocket. His socks matched his sweatband.

He looked like a warrior. He glanced at me with what was as close as you could come to a sneer without actual sneerage. Like I was an insect. In cutoffs.

Some people judge you just because your clothes are ratty and you have only one racket instead of fifteen. That gave me an advantage. I planned on surprising a few people.

"All right, gather round," the instructor said. He had on tight shorts, a tight shirt, shiny white shoes, and cologne I could have smelled from Utah. His hair was long and wavy—the kind you have to mousse five times a day. I guessed he was in his twenties. He had the shadow of a beard, and it looked like he actually shaved it that way.

I sensed a change in the girls. They stifled smiles, primped, looked at each other, whispered, and pretty much acted like Brad Pitt or Colin Farrell had plopped in front of them. When the instructor ran a hand through his hair, they gasped. It would have turned my stomach even if this guy hadn't almost killed us with his driving.

"I'm Guy Fornay. I'll be your instructor for the next two weeks."

Cue the swooning girls.

He called out names from a clipboard. The kid with the matching outfit was Maddox Ashworth. Guy tucked the clipboard under his arm and strutted like an army general. "This won't be the easiest two weeks of your life, but I promise you'll be better players by the end."

He introduced his high school help, then explained the singles and doubles tracks. Instruction was from 8 to 11, an hour for lunch, then a chalk talk, and a match hour where we'd play every other player or doubles pair.

"At the end of the two weeks there will be a tournament, and you can invite your family and friends."

I figured this was a way to get traffic into the country club to snag new members.

Guy called a few names, Ashley's and mine included, and told everyone else to go out onto the courts.

"I see that you haven't signed up for the meal plan," he said.

"I didn't know there was one," I said. It was probably a bag of chips, a sandwich, and a pickle for 50 bucks a day.

He looked at me like he recognized me from somewhere (a bug on his windshield?) and explained the meal program. Ashley and I were among the few who brought their own brown-bag lunches.

He shooed the rest away and turned to Ashley and me. "Didn't you see the camp guidelines for clothes? Tomorrow you need to be in proper tennis attire."

CHAPTER 5

❀ Ashley ❀

Guy was nice-looking, but I didn't care for his attitude. I wanted to tell him he needed to learn to drive too, but I held my tongue.

"How do we find out what proper attire is?" Bryce asked.

Guy cocked his head toward the other campers. "Collared shirt for you. Dress or skirt for you, preferably white. Shoes that won't scuff the courts."

"Do we have to buy the stuff in the pro shop?" Bryce said.

"If you want to be sure," he said.

As we walked onto the court, walkie-talkies squawked from the golf course. A long, motorized cart zipped past us, and I recognized the driver as Mr. Grassel, a man from our church. He was wearing a maintenance uniform. I waved but he must not have seen me.

"Wonder why he was going so fast," Bryce said.

"Something sure seemed wrong," I said.

Bryce caught up with Guy. "Do you have rules about going to the bathroom? Because I really have to go."

Guy frowned. "Make it quick."

Bryce gave me a wink as I headed onto the court. I knew what he was going to do.

CHAPTER 6

☺ *Bryce* ☺

I ran up the path to the pro shop, where the golfers check in and pay. Down a long hallway was the restaurant, and in between were the bathrooms. I passed the indoor tennis courts attached to the main building and hoped we'd get to play in there before camp was over.

Inside the pro shop were racks of shirts and lots of golf equipment collecting dust. Mr. Grassel huddled with another man in a suit. His name tag read Manager. They didn't seem to notice as I headed for the bathroom.

"A few more minutes and the whole thing would have been

ruined," Mr. Grassel was saying. "The sprinkler hits that stuff and
we're dead."

"Powdered grass killer?" the manager said.

"Yeah, if it had been liquid . . . I don't even want to think about
it. I used a vacuum to pick it up."

The manager's face was stern. He pointed in Mr. Grassel's face.
"This is the second time this has happened on your watch. We like
having you here, but—"

"Sir, I'm a groundskeeper, not a security guard. I told you when
the water lines were cut that we should have hired someone to
watch the place."

"But—" The manager noticed me peeking out of the bathroom
door and furrowed his brow. "Can we help you?"

"Uh, no, sir," I said, glancing at a bulletin board. There was an ad
for a used car, and I tore off one of the phone numbers. I went into
the bathroom, and when I came out they had moved outside.

CHAPTER 7

✖ Ashley ✖

I can think of only one word to sum up the first hour of tennis camp—*suicide*. That's the name of the first drill, and it separated the real players from the ones who mostly gasped. I felt like puking my guts out or, as Dylan would say, "tossing my Pop-Tarts."

The drill started with everyone at the back fence. Guy (who I was starting to seriously not like) blew his little whistle, and we ran to the baseline, then back to the fence, then farther to the service line, then back to the fence, then to the net and touched it, then raced to the fence. That's one suicide. It's supposed to increase our speed and endurance, but all it was doing was making me want to forget tennis camp and go home and watch TV while my legs recuperated.

We ran 10 suicides before Guy let us get a drink. It was warm on the court with the sun beating down. Summers in our part of Colorado are usually hot most of the day. (It's dry and the air is thin and doesn't make you feel like you're in a sauna like in Chicago.) The blue sky just stares at you as the sun crosses. People run their sprinklers early in the morning and late at night. If they don't, their grass shrivels, turns brown, and pretty soon even dogs don't pay attention.

The view from the courts was awe inspiring—if you didn't feel like heaving your breakfast. Pikes Peak looked like a brown crown in the distance, and a little closer was the Front Range, a line of mountains that looked like God's green fort.

"Isn't he cute?" Hayley said as she limped toward me.

"I'll let you know when I get some oxygen to my brain," I said.

Hayley complained about a blister on her heel, and I figured it was because she had new shoes. I grabbed a Band-Aid from my bag.

We ran and did foot drills for another 45 minutes. Then Guy and his high school buddies led hitting drills. We worked on nothing but our backhands the first hour, then our forehands. It looked to me like Guy was sizing up the talent pool.

The good players stood out like those rare paintings in elementary school hallways. You'll see a hundred pictures of dogs with round heads and stick-figure kids, then something that looks like it was drawn by a young Leonardo da Vinci. That's what the good players seemed like here. They walked differently, always had their rackets back in the ready position, ran drills effortlessly, and put the rest of us to shame.

I watched Bryce closely, and he didn't have the same skills as Maddox, the one who seemed the best. But Bryce is a fighter and picks things up fast. He was a whiz at the foot drills, started a little slow on the backhand drill, but by the end of the morning, I could tell he was catching on.

Clouds rolled in, which is another thing that often happens here. In the middle of the day, weather can cover the Front Range and move toward you like an angry army. It rains for an hour, and then it clears up. If you're climbing a mountain you have to do it early in the day so you don't get hit by lightning. I figured we'd move to the indoor courts once the clouds reached us.

Guy showed us drills we'd be doing the next day. Then he played king of the court. He divided us into four groups, each with a king. We took turns trying to score points and knock out the designated king on the other side.

I couldn't help hearing the kids at the pool splashing and laughing. I just wanted to go to lunch and take my shoes off.

CHAPTER 8

☺ *Bryce* ☺

Mad Dog Maddox ate up every shot fired at him.
I waited my turn, studying him, looking for any weakness. His forehand was lightning fast. He had a topspin backhand that jumped like a frog on steroids. His overhead was solid, his volleys crisp and tight, and he could hit a drop shot that landed inches from the net and bounced high enough for only a gnat to fly under.

"Cutoffs," Guy yelled at me, "you're next."

I stepped to the service line and felt butterflies in my stomach. Only these were more like tarantulas. Mad Dog crouched on the other side. My first serve plunked into the net, and I saw him move forward, as if protecting his kingdom was going to be a stroll by the moat. Second serve into the net. Double fault.

He had to win only two out of three points to keep his throne, so he didn't look worried when he hit his serve deep to my backhand. I figured I might as well pull out my surprise and hit the backhand as hard as I could. It skimmed the net, hit the line, and bounced twice to the fence. The king just stared.

Guy was talking with somebody and didn't see it. I heard Ashley shout, "Go, Bryce!"

It was the first point anyone had won from Mad Dog, and it made him look really mad. He poked at the strings in his racket and hopped from one foot to the other, awaiting my serve. This time it didn't go into the net. He returned it a little short, and I saw my chance. I hit a forehand deep to his backhand and rushed the net. It was the first time anyone had rushed the net on him too.

He saw what I was doing and hit a lob over my head that landed two inches inside the back line. I raced back to the fence, figuring Mad Dog was at the net, ready to return whatever weak shot I could muster. As the ball came down, I felt 30 pairs of eyes focused on our court.

Instead of lobbing it back and trying to get into better position, I decided to go for broke and hit a backhand with every ounce of strength I had left. I figured it would either rocket past him or he'd hit a drop shot and win.

CHAPTER 9

✖ Ashley ✖

In the back of my mind I was saying, *Bryce, pace yourself.* After all, this was the first day, and Bryce was taking on the tennis *wunderkind.*

When Bryce ran back, I thought he would lob the ball and get in position, but when he wound up for that backhand, I held my breath. He gritted his teeth and swung. Instead of the usual *thwop* of the ball against the strings, I head *plink.*

The ball hit the top of his racket and went straight up. Everybody shielded their eyes from the sun as it sailed and landed three courts down.

Maddox threw his head back and guffawed. Then the chuckles spread through the crowd. It *was* funny, but I could tell Bryce was in no mood to laugh. He shook his head, walked to the back of the line, and bonked his racket against the fence.

"Nice shot, Timberline," Duncan Swift yelled from the next court. He was king of that group, and I knew he was just trying to get Bryce to take things in stride. They had played enough sports together to become good friends, but from the look on Bryce's face, I could tell he wished Duncan had kept quiet.

Guy blew his whistle. "Meet back here at 12:15 or inside if it's raining."

I grabbed Bryce's tennis bag and handed it to him. "You'll get him next time."

He frowned. "Should have lobbed it."

CHAPTER 10

◑ *Bryce* ◑

The entrance to the country-club offices was on the other side of the building, so Ashley and I walked past the outdoor seating at the restaurant. I caught a whiff of sizzling bratwurst and hamburgers, and it made me think of the Colorado Rockies baseball stadium. I think they have the best food in baseball. Ashley says that even makes a 15–4 blowout enjoyable.

Not for me. I hate to lose.

We walked up the steps to the glass double doors, my muscles aching. A secretary told us Miss Davidson had to run to a meeting, "but she wanted me to give you something." The lady gave Ashley an envelope containing two tickets for lunch at the club, good for up to $10.

A note was tucked in with the tickets:

Dear Ashley and Brother (I can't remember your name),
Sorry I missed you. Hope you enjoy the camp and that these will make up for your inconvenience this morning.

Sincerely,
Jill Davidson

CHAPTER 11

❀ Ashley ❀

Bryce and I agreed that since we'd brought our lunches, we'd use the tickets the next day. Outside I spotted Hayley with Duncan Swift and waved, but she turned and laughed at something he said. I couldn't tell if she'd seen me or not, but I thought she had.

"Let's sit near the courts," Bryce said.

The bench wasn't comfortable, but it felt good just to sit. Somehow the peanut butter and jelly didn't taste as good as the food had smelled at the restaurant.

Golf carts puttered in the distance, and I watched a group of three men on a green, staring at a fourth. The fourth guy dinked the ball, then cursed and threw his putter when he missed a two-foot putt.

Men.

Another cart rolled up behind us, and Bryce waved. The driver, Mr. Grassel, slowed and squinted. "The Timberline twins," he said, parking just off the path. "How's tennis camp?"

I had seen Mr. Grassel at church and knew he and his wife had a son and daughter about Dylan's age. Something had gone wrong with the boy's birth, and now he had to have oxygen constantly. They wheeled around a little tank with plastic tubes that stuck in his nose. When he smiled at me, something inside me melted like the sun hitting an icy patch on the driveway.

"I saw you talking with that guy in the pro shop," Bryce said. "Something going on?"

"Yeah, we had some vandalism this morning. Somebody tried to mess up one of our greens, but I caught it. We had some sprinkler lines cut a few days ago. They want me to wave a magic wand and make it all go away, but for the life of me I can't understand why they haven't hired a security guard."

"Maybe they can't afford one," Bryce said.

Mr. Grassel nodded. "If I don't figure it out, I have a feeling they're going to let me go."

"They'll fire *you*?" I said. "That's not fair."

"Maybe not, but if we don't get a handle on this soon, the whole place will be shut down. Then it won't matter whether they fire me or anybody else."

CHAPTER 12

☺ *Bryce* ☺

Clouds hovered dark and ominous, kind of like the feeling I had about Mr. Grassel and what he was going through. Kids splashed in the pool, but I wondered how long the lifeguards would let them stay in.

"What are the chances someone from our tennis camp dropped the grass killer and cut the water lines?" Ashley said.

"What motive?" I said.

"Maybe someone doesn't want to run more suicides."

"Funny. They would have cut the nets."

She scrunched up her face.

"I don't like that look," I said. "It usually means you're hatching a plan."

"You don't like it because you didn't think of it first."

"What's the plan?"

"Get the names of all the kids in our camp and check them out."

"How are you going to do that?"

"Guy's clipboard. Should be simple. Then tonight we camp out near the course."

Thunder rumbled in the distance, and someone blew a whistle at the pool. Duncan and Hayley passed.

"Hey, Timberline," Duncan said. "Nice shot out there. You ought to go for court jester next time instead of king."

CHAPTER 13

❀ Ashley ❀

The indoor courts were nicer than the ones outside. You could look through a bunch of windows at anyone playing. Nice outfits hung on racks, and tennis rackets were for sale, as were mugs that said Red Rock Country Club. I looked at the prices, and they took my breath away.

Guy leaned against a counter, talking to a pretty woman. She smiled and giggled when she wasn't answering the phone.

The thunder grew louder, and I was glad we were inside.

I spotted Guy's clipboard with his rackets and gear at the bottom of the stairs, just outside the court. I moseyed down, trying to act relaxed. The clipboard had about 20 identical sheets, all listing the campers. I pulled one out and stuffed it in my shorts.

Guy gathered us on the court, informed us we'd be playing an eight-game set, and called out names and court numbers. We weren't in the first group, so Bryce and I sat in the lobby and tried to match names and faces from the list. I saw a lot of kids who looked like they might take their parents' credit cards to the mall and spend a billion dollars, but not many looked like they would vandalize a golf course.

When the first group finished, Guy called out, "Timberlines—you're playing Swift and Henderson."

CHAPTER 14

◒ *Bryce* ◒

Duncan is one of my best friends and a really good team-mate, but when we compete with each other, things can turn ugly. I remember a safe little game of Wiffle ball in our backyard last spring. We put up lawn chairs for bases and made up a bunch of rules, like if you throw the ball and hit a chair before the runner gets there, he's out. Duncan winged me not once but twice in the head with the ball. He said he was sorry, that it just got away from him, but I was ticked.

Duncan had last bat and won with a grand slam, 24–23. Walking back to the house, I could hardly breathe I was so mad. And that was only a Wiffle ball game with no one watching but my dogs, Pippin and Frodo.

"Ready to get stomped?" Duncan said, hitting three balls toward us. "You guys serve."

I knew Ashley liked him, and I knew Hayley was probably her best friend, so this was going to be a long set.

Ashley went to the net while I served. Hayley played the deuce court, Duncan the ad. In doubles it's important to get your first serve in and put the pressure on the other team. Some people try to hit their serves as hard as they can, but I've learned it's better to take some speed off the ball and just get it in.

Hayley hit a backhand that barely cleared the net, and Ashley moved to her right and hit the ball into the open court. Duncan anticipated the shot perfectly, took two steps back, and short hopped the ball back over. When I got to it, I noticed Hayley standing between the service line and the baseline, no-man's-land in tennis, and I hit the ball at her feet. She tried to block it, but it bounced off her racket out-of-bounds.

"That's okay," Duncan said, pounding his racket with his fist. "Come on. Let's go!"

He was trying to fire Hayley up, but he was really hacking me off. We weren't supposed to be out for blood, just working on fundamentals. Plus, we were friends.

I served to Duncan's backhand, which is his weakest shot. No way was I going to put a ball to Duncan's forehand, where he could blast it by Ashley down the line. He hit a soft shot over Ashley's head, and we switched courts. I made sure I kept the ball away from Duncan, and Hayley hit a lazy forehand that Ashley drilled at Duncan's feet.

Instead of saying, "Good shot," he stared at Ashley like she had kicked his puppy. "That the way you want to play?"

"Come on, Swift," I said.

He smashed the ball to me, all the way to the curtain backstop. I told Ashley to move to the baseline for my next serve. No sense in her getting drilled.

It's funny what happens when people get emotional about sports. Sometimes getting fired up makes you play better—more aggressively. But most of the time mad players do dumb things.

That's what Duncan did the rest of the set. He overswung, got mad at himself, cut in front of Hayley to intercept balls, only to hit them into the net. We won 8–2.

Ashley put an arm around Hayley as we walked off the court. Hayley's eyes were red.

Duncan slapped the cover on his racket and zipped it furiously.

"You were getting pretty hot out there," I said, trying to calm Duncan.

He stared at me. "I don't like to lose."

I could have said, "Get used to it," but I said, "By the end of this camp you two will be mopping the courts with us."

He nodded. "That's my goal."

Duncan was acting like a jerk, true, but he's not a Christian, and one thing I've learned is that you can't expect people to act like believers when they're not. Even Christians sometimes act like jerks. And a lot of these kids, it seemed, depended on how they did in sports to make them feel good about themselves.

CHAPTER 15

❋ Ashley ❋

I was glad it wasn't raining when we walked outside. In fact, the sun was out, and other than the wet concrete and the smell of rain, you couldn't tell we'd had a thunderstorm.

Hayley walked away from Duncan. I felt bad about beating them, but we really hadn't tried that hard. I also felt bad for being jealous about her playing with Duncan. I actually felt sorry for her.

It wasn't until she headed for the path behind the tennis courts that I got my idea. "Hayley, wait up!"

Her house backed up to the golf course. I didn't tell her why we wanted to, but I asked if she thought her mom would let Bryce and me camp out in their backyard that night.

Her face brightened. "Sounds fun. We could get two tents. You and me in one, Bryce in the other."

I joined Bryce at the ATVs. He studied the parking lot.

"Let me see that list," he said.

We watched parents pick up kids, others ride bikes, and a few walk home. Bryce wrote *C* for car, *B* for bike, and *W* for walker.

"The people who walk will be the best candidates, but it could be anybody," he said. "The only way we're going to find out is if we get to know some of the kids."

Two men in suits came out of the country club. They stopped in the parking lot and talked. One guy pointed at the other, who shook his head a lot.

CHAPTER 16

☺ *Bryce* ☺

At home I just wanted to find a cool place in the house and take a nap, especially if we were going to camp out in Hayley's backyard (which wasn't a sure thing).

"Sam and I have decided not to go to the memorial service this year," Mom said.

Ever since our real dad died, there's been an annual service for family members near where the crash took place. At least, as near to the ocean as you can get without actually going in. It was at one of those services that Mom met Sam. There are always lots of people crying and throwing flowers in the water and government officials with serious faces. Ashley and I hadn't been to every service, but

Mom had, and it seemed a little like we were betraying Dad not to have someone there.

"Why?" I said.

"There are things going on," Mom said. "That's all."

She got a far-off look, and I glanced at Ashley. Sometimes she knows more about what's going on with Mom and Sam than I do because . . . well, she pays more attention and talks a lot with Mom. But Ashley looked like she didn't have a clue.

Ashley said, "You and Sam aren't having trouble, are you?"

Mom rolled her eyes, grabbed a stalk of celery, and went wild with her knife. "Nothing like that. It's just . . . we'll talk about it more when Sam comes home."

Sam had been on the phone a lot lately. Before he married Mom, he was in some elite antiterrorist military group, which is why the terrorists blew up the plane he was supposed to be on. The plane our dad was on. It's a long story, and by the way Mom talked, the whole thing hadn't been told yet.

We couldn't drag anything more out of Mom, so Ashley asked if we could sleep over at Hayley's house. Mom said yes pretty fast, which made me think she was glad to change the subject.

We packed our stuff, and I went through my closet to find an outfit that would please Guy. Ashley had a tennis dress from the year before, with those frilly shorts. I told her it made her rear end look like SpongeBob SquarePants, but I don't think she took that as a compliment.

I could hear Mom and Leigh, our stepsister, shouting downstairs. Leigh's going to be a senior in high school this fall and wants to drive her own car to school. She had found a car in the paper, and Mom was saying something about getting Sam involved. Things weren't going well.

I went downstairs, rummaged through my pocket, pulled out a wadded piece of paper, and handed it to Leigh.

"What's this?" she said, like I was a skunk who had just walked into her slumber party.

"Found it on a bulletin board at the country club." I closed my eyes and quoted the ad. "'Honda Accord. Four-door. Good condition. Silver. Great back-to-school car. $1,500.'"

Leigh looked at me like I had changed from a skunk to a knight in shining armor. "Think it's still for sale?"

"If it's on the bulletin board, it's probably up for grabs."

Leigh cradled the crumpled number like it was a winning lottery ticket. "I'm going to call, just to see if they still have it."

Mom said, "I still want Sam in on this."

CHAPTER 17

❀ Ashley ❀

I was sure Hayley had nothing to do with destroying the golf course, but Bryce suggested we not tell her what we were doing. He said he wanted to fly under the radar and try to solve the mystery without tipping off anyone.

At Hayley's house we parked our ATVs at the edge of the country-club parking lot. People were hitting at the outdoor court, and the lights were on indoors as well. A group of golfers straggled to the clubhouse, looking tired. We walked next to the 18th-hole tee box, and Bryce pointed out tees all over the ground.

"Why wouldn't they pick them up?" I said.

"They do at the first hole. By the time they get to the 18th, they're too tired to bend over. That's why you can find all kinds of lost balls around the 18th hole too. At least that's what Sam says."

Hayley's mom had made lemonade, and her dad had the grill going in the backyard. We played badminton while we waited. Bryce pretended to be Duncan and kept Hayley laughing. He'd serve the birdie, run under the net and return his own serve, then run back, push me out of the way, and hit the thing again. When he missed, he showed his teeth and sneered like Duncan. I was laughing so hard I was afraid I was going to wet my pants.

After dinner Bryce set up the tents while Hayley took me inside. I showed her my old tennis dress, and she said she had something that would be a lot better. She opened her closet, and I thought I had died and gone to the Gap. She said I could wear her new outfit if I wanted, but I chose a different one.

Duncan was the elephant in the room—you know, the thing you know you should talk about, that you both are thinking about, but you're too scared to talk about. After a few minutes of trying on clothes, the whole Duncan thing faded and we just had fun.

When we got back outside, Bryce and Hayley's dad were playing horseshoes, so we sat and watched in the fading light. A fox loped across the fairway near us, sniffing at the wind. I guessed he wanted some of the hamburgers, and Hayley grabbed a hot dog her dad had dropped on the ground and tossed it. The fox bit it and ran away. I wasn't sure that was good for the fox, but I figured there was a grateful bunny in the bushes somewhere.

We roasted marshmallows in a fire pit. Out of the blue Bryce said, "Why don't we have our own service?"

"What are you talking about?" Hayley said.

I explained what Mom had said about the memorial service.

Hayley has been to our church a few times, but I'm still not sure where she is with God. Some things had happened in the past few months that made me think she was more interested than not.

"What does your mom mean about stuff going on?" Hayley said.

I shrugged. "There's a lot they never tell us."

Bryce finished a perfectly toasted marshmallow. "We could go to Red Rock Lake, read some verses. Do our own thing."

"I bet your dad would appreciate it," Hayley said. "Do you think he can hear or see the stuff you're doing?"

"I'm not sure," I said. "There's a verse in the Bible that makes me think people who have died can see things going on down here. Having a service of our own seems like a good idea to me too. Anything we can do to keep Dad's memory alive sounds good."

CHAPTER 18

◕ *Bryce* ◕

I had forgotten Sam's night-vision gadget, so I walked back along the nearby fairway to the ATVs. The moon was already up, and I didn't have a problem finding my way, so long as I stayed in the middle of the fairway. At the edges, under the trees, it was dark. I wondered if animals hid in there, waiting to jump out.

I stood at the tee box on the first hole, the best view of the course, and watched for any movement. Someone was running after a dog across fairway #2, but that was all.

As I moved past the country club, I noticed a second-floor light. Maybe somebody was figuring out a way to save the club.

The nightscope was in a locked case fastened to the back of my ATV. I keep my wallet, a flashlight, and some first-aid stuff in there just in case. Through the scope I could see into the shadows of the parking lot. I glanced up at the country club and saw someone move out of sight in one of the windows.

As I crossed the road near the tennis courts, something snorted. An animal. A big one. Signs nearby warned about bears getting into garbage cans. I'd had a run-in with a bear a few weeks before, and I didn't want to repeat that.

I stopped and scanned the area. What if Ashley and Hayley had followed me and were trying to scare me? It was working.

I headed back toward Hayley's house, using the scope to look around. It cast a weird green tint, and I found I could walk as long as I had one eye to the scope and the other open.

I made it back to Hayley's house and the backyard fire. "You guys been here the whole time?"

Ashley looked at me like I had an extra arm. "'Course. Why?"

CHAPTER 19

✖ Ashley ✖

Hayley and I crawled into our tent. I felt kind of bad that Bryce was alone in his, but he didn't seem to mind. He was going to stay awake and watch the golf course, but we hadn't taken into account how many acres the place covered. With the scope, Bryce could see through a flap at the back of his tent, but I wondered how much good we were going to do.

I figured I'd wait until Hayley went to sleep and then join Bryce or maybe take a walk, but Hayley wanted to talk. I pretended to yawn and hoped she'd get tired, but when she finally brought up Duncan, I was awake.

"I couldn't believe he asked me to play," Hayley said. "My mom and his mom are friends, so maybe they suggested it."

"He's so competitive," I said. "If he'd just wanted to play, he would have been in the singles track, don't you think? He probably has a thing for you."

"You should have heard him talking about you and Bryce before we started. He was going over all the possible teams we might play, telling me how we'd match up. He said the best is that Ashworth kid and his partner, Tiffany, but that you and Bryce were a close second."

"So he thought you'd lose to us?"

"I don't think *lose* is in his vocabulary." She rolled over in her sleeping bag and propped herself up on her elbows. "You're not mad at me because I didn't tell you about this, are you? I mean, he only asked me yesterday."

I shook my head. "I don't ever want some guy to come between us."

CHAPTER 20

⊙ *Bryce* ⊙

A giant fox chased me with a giant hot dog hanging out of his mouth. I ran toward a huge golf flag, grabbed it, and rode it like a fireman's pole. The fox sniffed, scratched, and tried to get at me, but I hunkered down.

That's when I woke up. I thought I heard growling, but I figured that was my imagination.

The last thing I remembered was Ashley and Hayley giggling and then feeling really tired. The nightscope lay next to me.

I dug through my sleeping bag to find my watch. No luck. Pain shot through my leg and up my whole body. I'd had muscle cramps before, but this was the mother of all cramps, and it was all I could do not to scream.

I felt like I'd been run over by a garbage truck. We had talked in science class about why muscles get sore. Our teacher said when we exercise, our muscles produce lactic acid, and that's what makes you sore. She said you're sore until the acid goes away. I asked her what happened if you were lactic-acid intolerant, but she didn't think it was as funny as the rest of us did. Now I felt like I'd been dunked in lactic acid and left to soak.

Something revved in the distance—probably the growling sound I had heard. I sat straight up and ignored the pain. That engine sounded like an ATV.

I grabbed the nightscope and hobbled outside. The night air was cool, and a billion stars lit the sky. Security lights clicked on at the back of Hayley's house. The engine revved again, like it was bogged down.

A dog barked. Then another picked up the message and passed it on, and pretty soon half a dozen joined the dog chorus.

I got a sick feeling in my stomach, and it wasn't lactic acid. I pulled out my flashlight and fumbled through my backpack.

The keys to my ATV weren't there.

CHAPTER 21

❀ Ashley ❀

"What is it?" I said when Bryce shook me awake. Sleeping on the ground hadn't helped my pain. I felt like a 90-year-old woman.

"I'm not sure," he whispered. "Come on."

Hayley slept as I slipped on my shoes and crept away. Bryce had his flashlight out, and we stayed in the middle of the fairway. By the time we reached the country club, I didn't feel nearly as stiff.

"I thought I heard an ATV or a motorcycle," Bryce said, panting. "And if I'm right . . ." He pointed the flashlight to where we had parked our ATVs. "No!"

"What?" I said, squinting into the darkness.

He ran a bit farther and I saw.

"Mine's gone," he said. "I must have left my keys here when I came for the nightscope."

"Then let's call—"

He put his fingers over my mouth. "Listen."

"I don't hear anything."

"Exactly."

He took off toward the country club with me close at his heels. I almost tripped on a speed bump but managed to navigate onto the sidewalk. At the back of the club overhead lights showed the path. We sprinted up the other side to the outdoor courts. Bryce cut through a practice green and down a hill to the next hole. He stopped and we both listened.

"Bryce, we should call the police," I whispered.

"It sounded bogged down, like it was stuck." Bryce turned. "Remember when Sam brought us out here? Which hole was it that had the par three over water—the one you bogeyed?"

I didn't remember every hole or every score I'd ever had, but I remembered that one. I hit the ball way right. It bounced on the hill and rolled down next to the green. I three putted for a bogey.

"It was on the front nine," I said. "Wasn't it the sixth?"

He nodded and darted onto the fairway. I jogged behind him, trying to keep my footing. The sprinklers had been going, and the ground sloshed. We crossed a bridge over a stream, where I had lost at least four balls one day.

"Six is that way," Bryce said.

We cut through some trees and tall grass. I noticed something to our left. Bryce pointed the flashlight, but the beam wasn't strong enough.

"It looks like somebody running!" I said.

Bryce aimed his nightscope. He shook his head. "Looked like a jogger on the road up there."

We kept going until we came to the cart path that wound around some pine trees and a hill. The moon didn't give enough light to see much in the valley. Bryce put his nightscope to one eye, and his shoulders sagged.

CHAPTER 22

☺ *Bryce* ☺

I couldn't believe my ATV was stuck in three feet of water at
the edge of a pond. Someone had driven it straight across the green,
leaving deep tire tracks. I didn't know which made me madder—
that they would steal my ATV or that they would tear up the course
for fun.

I handed the scope to Ashley and she gasped. "Why would
anyone do that?"

I waded out to the ATV and tried to start it. The thing was so deep
in the muck that I knew Ashley and I would never be able to push it
out.

I thought of Mr. Grassel and his family and all the other workers at the country club. We had tried to help, and now my ATV had been used to damage part of the course.

We raced back and woke Hayley. I called the police from her house. A few minutes later Hayley's dad came downstairs and didn't look happy. I kept apologizing for leaving my keys in the ATV.

Somebody must have called our house, because Sam soon showed up and took us home.

CHAPTER 23

✖ Ashley ✖

I woke up to Dylan hovering over me, smiling, with strawberry Pop-Tarts crumbs all over his face. "Ashley's up!" he shouted.

I tickled him and rolled out of bed. We'd had a late night, but Bryce and I didn't want to miss a minute of camp. It really had our attention now. I dressed in Hayley's outfit and raced downstairs.

Bryce and I whispered about our plan for the day and possible suspects. I thought the missing ATV had something to do with the mysterious jogger. "Who goes jogging after midnight?"

Sam drove us to the country club and dropped us off. A Red Rock police car sat in the parking lot, and next to the country club entrance was Bryce's muddy and dripping ATV. Mr. Grassel unhooked a chain from it.

"You don't know how bad I feel," Bryce said.

Mr. Grassel looked grim. "I'm really disappointed. I never thought you would do something like this."

"You think Bryce did it?" I said.

Mr. Grassel pursed his lips. "This is your machine. You were camping nearby. Who else?"

A police officer came out of the pro shop and headed for us.

"They think *we* had something to do with it?" I said.

Bryce shook his head. "Not *we*. Me."

"That's crazy."

"They must think I took the thing out last night, got it stuck, and then called the police to try and cover myself."

"I was with you the whole time."

A car with a funny-looking insignia on the front pulled up and parked in the handicap spot outside the country club. A man in a suit jumped out, and I recognized him from the day before. "I'm the manager," he told the officer. "Are these the two?"

A bunch of kids watched now, and I felt my face flush. Maddox stepped out of an expensive car with all his rackets.

"I want them in the office right now," the manager said.

"I don't have anything to hide," Bryce said.

My knees shook—not because I was guilty, but because of how mad everybody looked.

Inside I was surprised to see Hayley and her father. She was crying.

CHAPTER 24

☺ *Bryce* ☺

I couldn't believe they were accusing me of wrecking the golf course, especially after all the ways we'd helped the Red Rock police in the past few months. I kept telling myself they were just doing their jobs and that the country club was in a bind, but it ticked me off.

They took Ashley and Hayley into another room. The office door was open, and people walked by and looked at me like I was a criminal. Through the back window I could barely see the sixth hole over the trees. It looked like a construction site for a tunnel project.

I wondered what my real dad would have said. Most likely, "Just tell them the truth, Son."

The police officer led me to a room where the club manager sat.

"I've been talking with your sister and her friend," the officer said. "We have a good idea what happened last night, and it would be a lot better for you if you'd tell us what you did, straight up."

I looked the officer right in the eyes. It's scary talking to any adult who thinks you've done something bad, but especially one in a uniform with a gun on his hip.

I told him Ashley and I had found out about the vandalism at the golf course and wanted to find clues. I told him about going for the nightscope and leaving the keys, but I didn't mention the snort I had heard.

The officer leaned forward. "Your sister says you woke her up."

"Yeah, I heard the ATV revving and went to get her."

"Sure you hadn't just got back from your little joyride? Then you took your sister on a wild-goose chase when you knew exactly where that ATV was?"

The manager leaned in, pointing at me. "Do you know how much it's going to cost to repair the damage?"

"I didn't do it," I said as firmly as I could. "We saw some guy running by the road as we headed out to number six."

"Midnight jogger?" the manager scoffed.

"Bryce, we all make mistakes," the officer said. "If we walk out of here and you don't tell us exactly what happened, it's not going to be good for you."

The *thwop* of tennis balls echoed from the courts. I looked the man in the eyes again and felt my voice quiver. "Ask anybody who knows me. I don't destroy people's property. I was out there trying to help."

The officer let me go back into the other room.

"I tried to convince them, but they wouldn't listen," Ashley said.

"Where's Hayley?"

"They let her go."

Jill Davidson walked in and leaned down, furrowing her brow. "I heard what happened. Is there anything I can do?"

"Convince them I didn't do it," I said.

She walked into the next room, leaving the door open. I heard the cop use the words *impound* and *press charges.*

Then Jill spoke clearly, like she wanted us to hear her. "I met these kids yesterday. You should be looking for who stole the ATV rather than accusing him."

The door closed quickly, and Ashley and I looked at each other.

Finally the police officer came out. His face was drawn tight as he walked toward me. "This is your last chance. Tell us the truth and—"

"I already told you the truth," I said.

The officer nodded. "We're impounding your ATV as evidence. You'll hear from us soon."

The manager walked past us. "Get that other vehicle off country-club property. You're forbidden to drive those things here."

CHAPTER 25

❀ Ashley ❀

I was glad Bryce and I were late to tennis camp, because it looked like everyone had done more suicides. Guy taught the correct way to hit an overhead, showing us racket preparation, how to point at the ball, when to let the ball hit the court and when to hit it out of the air—that kind of thing. He hit several overheads, and each one of them stuck in the fence at the back of the courts. I didn't see Hayley and wondered if she had gone home with her father.

Guy finally saw us and everyone got quiet. "So, the Timberlines have graced us with their presence. Care to tell us why you're late?"

"A little misunderstanding at the country club," Bryce said.

The kids snickered and whispered among themselves.

"Well, I don't appreciate tardiness. Go to the end court and run 10 suicides."

My mouth dropped. "But they were the ones who made us late."

"Doesn't matter," Guy said. "Ten suicides, full-out. Whoever comes in second has to do 10 more."

Bryce tapped me on the shoulder. "Come on."

I could tell Bryce wasn't going top speed. He slowed and let me catch him, and when we finished our 10th one, I reached the back fence before him.

Guy was there as we bent double, hands on knees. "I said full-out. That wasn't as fast as you can go. Both of you do 10 more."

I was too tired to protest. Bryce and I put our backs to the fence while he blew the whistle. We did 10 more suicides until it felt like we were going to heave our breakfasts.

We finished as he called for the group to take a break. Bryce and I grabbed water bottles and stumbled outside the fence to a grassy knoll above the courts. From there we could see the town of Red Rock, Pikes Peak in the distance, and even our middle school with the climbing wall beside it.

"I hate this place," I said. "I wish we'd never signed up."

"If I hadn't left my key, none of this would've happened."

"Don't blame yourself. What that person did is a crime. Why do you think they tried to frame you?"

"Maybe they don't like us nosing around," Bryce said. He stared at something on the ground. "Look at that."

All around the knoll were holes, places someone had dug with a shovel then covered haphazardly.

"Why would anybody dig out here?" Bryce said.

"Maybe burying something?"

I scooped some dirt out and examined it. It was almost like sand. "Hope they're burying bombs to destroy the place."

Bryce looked at me. "We're on to something. No giving up until we figure out what it is."

Guy blew his whistle, and I thought about giving up on the tennis camp and heading for the pool. "Okay," I said. "And let's beat Maddox and Tiffany when we get the chance."

CHAPTER 26

☺ *Bryce* ☺

Ashley and I finished the morning session spent of energy but eager to get to the restaurant. We had our vouchers out and ready as we went through the line. We chose chips, drinks, and desserts along with our burgers. I knew the food would sit heavy in our stomachs, but it was paid for.

The problem was finding a place to sit. As we came through, several kids scooted over to make it look like they didn't have room. We finally found a table in the corner that hadn't been cleaned. I was glad Ashley was with me, because it's terrible to be shunned *and* alone.

Ashley went to find mustard. I had a full mouth when Maddox approached. "I heard about what you did."

"The ATV was mine, but I didn't trash the course."

He nodded. "My dad thinks you did. He knows the manager."

"Well, he doesn't know me. I'd never do that."

Maddox pawed at the chair, so I asked if he wanted to sit. He shook his head. "I was thinking, you and your sister are pretty good. Want to come to my house and play sometime? We have a court of our own."

I had a hard time swallowing my burger and an even harder time believing what I was hearing. "Sure," I said.

He told me where he lived. "How about Saturday?"

CHAPTER 27

✖ Ashley ✖

Bryce said it would be a good opportunity to snoop around. "Maddox doesn't live far from here. He could have been the one who stole my ATV or planted the grass killer."

"Then why would he invite us to his house, especially after telling you his father thinks you're guilty?"

Bryce shrugged. "You know, that crime-and-punishment thing."

"No."

"Well, I guess there's this book called *Crime and Punishment*, and the guy who commits the crime feels so guilty that he tries to get caught."

"Great, you've ruined the ending."

"Maybe Maddox feels bad about me being accused and wants to make it up to me."

That afternoon the singles players hit the outside courts, and we played doubles inside against Lou and Leslie Bolan. They were twins too, a year older than us, and they looked like a synchronized swimming duo on the court. They flashed hand signals behind their backs, yelled "Help!" or "Switch" during our returns, and when they'd win a point they had a special high five.

They had everything going for them—except they were really bad. Bryce hit Leslie a hard shot at the net, and you'd have thought she'd broken a nail. She held the racket up to protect herself, and the ball missed her by three feet. When Lou served, he lifted his right leg, and I couldn't help thinking of our dogs, Pippin and Frodo. The two only high-fived each other half a dozen times, and that was because Bryce and I made some silly mistakes.

They were sweet, though, and good losers. Sometimes you play people who throw their rackets and curse and make it look like you never *win* a point, that they just *lose.* But Lou and Leslie complimented us every time we aced them or hit a winner.

"There're two people we don't have to worry about messing with the golf course," I said as we waited for Mom to pick us up. "Squeaky clean."

"You never know," Bryce said.

Mr. Grassel passed us on his cart. We waved but he just nodded. I guess he had reason to think we were part of the problem instead of the solution. I hoped we'd be able to help him before our two weeks were up.

CHAPTER 28

☺ *Bryce* ☺

We'd left our tents at Hayley's house, so Sam drove us to pick them up. Things were pretty tense. When we got home, Leigh was excited about the car I'd told her about. She had phoned the owner.

"We've set up a meeting tomorrow afternoon at the country club to look at it."

"Who's the owner?" I said.

"Some man named Guy."

Ashley and I looked at each other.

I flipped on the television news and saw a man talking about a plane crash. The graphic behind him had the flight number of my real dad's plane. I turned it up just as he was saying, ". . . startling new information on a deadly plane crash, when we come back."

Leigh stopped talking about the car and focused on the TV. It seemed the toilet-paper and nasal-spray commercials would never end, but finally the man came back and introduced another reporter.

"As we near the anniversary of the deadly crash that took hundreds of lives, families and friends of the victims now have one more thing to add to their grief. Their loved ones' deaths may not have been caused by a terrorist. It may simply have been an accident."

CHAPTER 29

✖ Ashley ✖

I couldn't breathe. They flashed pictures of pilots, flight atten-
dants, and passengers.

"There's Mom!" Leigh said, covering her mouth.

Every picture of the rescue crews, the boats picking up wreckage,
the grim faces of waiting family members brought back old feelings.
Bryce and I had been in school, about to go to lunch, when a neighbor picked us up. There were whispers and nervous glances by the
office staff as we walked outside. I told them we weren't supposed
to go with anyone but our parents, but the neighbor assured us she
was taking us home.

There were lots of cars in our driveway, and even though we asked many times what was going on, our neighbor would only say, "Your mother needs you home, Ashley."

We walked through a gauntlet of people at the house. Most of them were crying. Some had brought food. I recognized a few of Dad's golfing friends and some from his church. It felt like an hour before we found Mom and she knelt to hug us.

"What's wrong?" Bryce said. "Why are all these people here?"

She stroked his hair, and we walked hand in hand up to her room. Dylan slept in his crib. "Something terrible has happened to your father," she said. "You know he went on a trip today."

"To England on business," Bryce said.

"Well, something happened to the plane. They think it might have been terrorists—a man has taken responsibility for the crash."

"The plane crashed?" I said, trying to hold back the tears. "Like 9/11?"

She hugged us tight and said something about things happening that we don't understand. Bryce and I pulled away and asked her the truth.

"There were no survivors. Dad's not coming home."

Later that night I asked Mom if Dad was in heaven, and she said she was sure he was. Then I asked if we would see him again, and she hesitated. She wasn't a Christian back then, so I guess she wasn't sure. But she finally said, "Yes, I think we'll see him again."

Now the TV flashed a photo of the terrorist, Asim bin Asawe, and it brought me back to the present. My mind reeled so much I didn't catch it all, but the new finding said the crash might have been a problem with the airplane's fuel tank. Even though witnesses reported seeing a streak of light going toward the plane, this new finding said it might have just been an accident.

In one sense, it didn't make a difference whether it was an attack or an accident. Either way our dad was dead. But in another sense, it made a big difference. That it was a terrorist gave us hope that the person responsible would someday be caught and punished. That it might have been an accident gave me a hollow feeling.

CHAPTER 30

☺ Bryce ☺

Sam rushed in—he'd heard the report on the radio. His wife and young daughter had been killed in that crash. His whole life had turned upside down thinking it was this terrorist, and now the authorities had a different theory?

He said he had been in contact with Washington, that there were things he couldn't tell us, and that the news media didn't know everything.

Great, I thought. *More mystery.*

Leigh asked if Sam could take her to the country club the next day to look at a car, and when he said he'd have to check his schedule she stomped off to her room.

I guess we all were bummed about the news.

CHAPTER 31

✖ Ashley ✖

Bryce and I were almost late to tennis camp the next day, and we hurried Mom so we wouldn't have to do extra suicides. We got stares and funny looks from a lot of the kids, but I wasn't as sore and Guy tried out some new drills. Three of us would get in one corner, three in another, and Guy (or one of the high schoolers) threw balls to our forehands. Whoever got closest to the target on the other side of the net won and got to move to the next court.

At lunch Bryce and I moved to a bench by the outdoor courts. I'd forgotten to take my medicine that morning and had thrown both bottles of pills into my tennis bag. I have a seizure disorder that my doctor hopes I'll grow out of. I have to take medicine every morning and every night so my brain doesn't do weird things. It's kind of scary, but I've gotten used to the meds.

A few high school helpers ate nearby, talking about their rankings, the upcoming season, and their biggest competition. A long-haired guy rode up on his bicycle and sat down.

A tall, skinny guy said he was going to use the money he made from teaching at the camp to buy a new racket. Another said he was going to use his on a vacation to some island.

Someone else said he'd been saving for a car, but he was way short of what he needed. "You guys have any idea where I could make some more dough?"

"I've got an idea," the long-haired guy said, "but I'm not telling you losers."

"Sean's got an idea?" Skinny laughed. "That's a first. He'd better get rid of it before it gets lonesome."

"Wait and see," Sean said. "I'm going to be rolling in it while you guys are still chasing tennis balls."

CHAPTER 32

☺ *Bryce* ☺

Ashley and I won our doubles match that afternoon against a good team. They played well but hit a lot of balls short, and Ashley and I pounced on them.

Afterward, we waited by the pro shop where Mom was supposed to pick us up. Instead, Sam and Leigh drove up. Guy met them halfway to the parking lot.

I noticed the old Honda and wondered what Guy was doing driving both an ultraexpensive car and a clunker. Sam came over and told us he and Leigh were going for a test-drive.

Guy gave them the keys and let them drive off.

While Ashley and I were waiting inside, the manager came in and handed the cashier a bag. It looked full. The cashier said he would put it in the safe and take it the next morning on his weekly run to the bank. The manager glanced at us.

"So you're getting rid of your old car," the cashier said to Guy. "How many miles on it?"

Guy told him 187,000, and the man whistled. "You have the timing belt changed?"

"Yeah, at 100,000," Guy said. "It's in good shape. Brakes need work, but it's a good deal."

It's funny watching your older stepsister make a car deal. When she and Sam returned, Leigh chuckled at the things she noticed that were wrong. The rearview mirror hung by a thread, and one of the side mirrors was cracked. Sam seemed uninterested at first, but then I saw him studying Guy.

"I'd like to get it checked out at our local shop tomorrow," Leigh said. "The brakes made a noise."

"Probably just a little dry," Guy said. "But sure, that's fine. You want to pick it up here or at my apartment in town?"

"Here's fine," Leigh said.

Leigh was giggly going home, which was not like her. She even asked how our tennis camp was going.

"Good decision about having it checked out," Sam said.

"I can't wait to tell Randy about the car. I bet he'll look at it for me."

CHAPTER 33

✿ Ashley ✿

Randy is Leigh's boyfriend. Bryce and I used to call him The Creep, but not anymore. He's been coming to our church lately, and not just because he wants to play on the softball team. He seems interested.

Randy pulled up and Leigh ran out to him. Bryce asked if I wanted to volley some in the backyard, but I couldn't find my tennis bag. Then I realized I had left it at the club.

"That's okay. I can use an old racket from the barn," Bryce said.

"But my medicine's in there! I have to get it."

Mom had gone to a meeting at church, and Sam was about to

take me when Randy volunteered. Bryce and I waited a long time while he and Leigh talked. It was dark when we set out.

The Colorado Rockies were on the radio, so Randy stayed in his truck to listen as Bryce and I went to the indoor courts. My heart sank when I saw the dark country club. The lights at the outdoor courts were out too.

"I should have called," I said.

"We could call Mr. Grassel," Bryce said. "He probably has a key."

There was a light on just outside the indoor courts. Bryce went to the door, and it opened.

We walked gingerly inside. The lights above the courts were on, but the lobby was dark.

"Hello?" I called. "Anybody here?"

"Strange," Bryce said. "Everything else is locked but this. Where did you leave your bag?"

I pointed to court #5. My yellow bag hung on a bench beside the net.

It was creepy walking around an unlocked building that should have been shut tight. We moved down the stairs to the court door. Before we could open it, something banged and echoed through the hallway.

"What was that?" I whispered.

"Could be the tennis fairy, but don't bet on it."

If my heart hadn't been racing 300 beats a minute I would have laughed. We waited, thinking someone would yell at us for trespassing. If the manager heard we were here after hours, he would have us kicked out of the camp.

"Get your stuff," Bryce said. "I'll wait here."

"No way. Come with me."

Bryce got a faraway look in his eye. "Isn't the tennis club connected to the pro shop? You can get to it through that hallway, can't you?"

"Why?"

"Because if those doors are open, anybody could steal rackets and shirts and equipment."

"Just come with me to the court, okay?"

CHAPTER 34

☾ *Bryce* ☾

I followed Ashley through the doors and behind the curtain that ran the length of the courts. It's a long, green plastic thing that hangs from the ceiling to keep the balls from rolling to the wall. You have to hit it a few times to see where the break is so you can go through.

Just as Ashley ran onto court #5, I heard creaking metal behind us, like a door being opened. Ashley froze and looked at me.

"Hello?" I said, and my voice got lost in the cavernous building. My mind raced. I shuffled over to Ashley as she grabbed her tennis bag.

"Do you have your phone?" Ashley said.

I felt my front pocket. No. "Didn't think I'd need it." I grabbed a tennis ball and threw it hard at the far wall. It cleared the top of the green curtain by inches and clattered down the other side.

"Anybody there?" I yelled.

Ashley moved closer. "Let's get out of here."

Before we could move, the lights went out.

CHAPTER 35

❀ Ashley ❀

If you've never experienced pitch-darkness, try going into a closet at midnight. It's like having your eyes taped shut. Now take yourself out of the closet into a huge building with nets and curtains and stairs and doors that you're not familiar with, and you can imagine what we felt like.

I grabbed Bryce's shirt as someone moved behind the curtain. It sounded like they stumbled over tennis balls. I couldn't tell which way they were moving, but I knew which way I wanted to go. The courts had long netting between them, so I pulled Bryce toward the back curtain, and we smacked it until we found the opening.

Big steel girders stuck out from the wall. We moved toward the lobby doors, trying not to trip on errant tennis balls. I couldn't tell if the person who had turned off the lights was behind us, ahead of us, or had gone somewhere else.

We finally reached the lobby doors and stumbled up the steps. We couldn't tell where the furniture was, so we dropped and crawled along the carpet.

Suddenly the front door burst open and someone darted out.

"Did you see who it was, Bryce?"

"No."

When the door closed we were in darkness again, but we had seen the direction of the stairs. We made it to the outer door, and Bryce hit it. The security light outside lit the sidewalk, and it felt like we had come up from a deep-sea dive and gasped the first breath of air.

"Run that way and look," Bryce said.

I didn't want to run anywhere but back to the parking lot, but I made it to the end of the building and peeked around the corner. Several other outside lights were on, but I didn't see anyone.

I went back and found Bryce running up the incline to the parking lot. A car streaked from the rear lot and didn't slow at the stop sign. Whoever was driving kept the lights off.

CHAPTER 36

☻ *Bryce* ☻

Back in the car we asked Randy if he had seen anyone come from the tennis center. He turned the radio down and said, "What?"

When we told him what happened he ran around the club, making sure no one was still there. We borrowed his cell phone. I didn't want the police accusing me of breaking in, so we called home and asked Sam for Mr. Grassel's number.

Mr. Grassel arrived at the country club in 15 minutes. Ashley explained what we were doing there and what had happened. He scowled as we walked toward the tennis center.

We went through the building with him. He checked the door
that led to the country club and found it locked. He led us behind
the green curtain and pulled back a plastic covering to reveal a safe.

"Closed," Mr. Grassel said. "Looks secure. Still, I'll need to report
this. The police can get in touch with you if they need to. And hey,
thanks for telling us. Other kids might not have said anything. Good
job."

CHAPTER 37

✖ Ashley ✖

Sam's office is on the second floor of our old barn, and he has a killer view of Pikes Peak. Around the room are little airplanes and helicopter statues and paintings, several filing cabinets, and a huge chair. He had a steaming cup of coffee on the desk and was just hanging up the phone when Bryce and I entered before tennis camp the next morning.

Sam can hold a gaze a long time, and I was the one who broke the uncomfortable silence. "They never told us *how* it happened, *how* the plane went down." I paused. "And what happened to the passengers. I've always imagined it was some kind of missile, or a piece of luggage exploded and the plane just dropped into the water. That the passengers didn't feel anything."

Sam sucked his upper lip down, and his lower lip covered part of his mustache.

Bryce said, "We figured if anybody would know, you would."

Part of growing up is asking hard questions and being willing to hear the answers. Until now, I'd been too scared to listen, wanting to go "Na na na" and plug my ears. But part of my childhood was dying, and there was no way to stop it.

Sam leaned back in his chair and rubbed his face. He looked out the back window to the red rock formation behind our house. He took a swig of his coffee. "I always imagined someone sitting next to my wife and daughter and taking care of them in those last few moments. Someone who made it a little easier. About a year ago I got the passenger list—the seating chart. Your dad was in the row behind them."

Wow! What were the odds?

"Why haven't you asked your mother about this?" he said.

"We didn't want to upset her," Bryce said. "Maybe we didn't really want to know. But now, with the news report . . ."

He nodded. "I've been in some pretty hairy situations in the air. I imagine it was pretty bad up there."

"Why are they saying it's mechanical now and not a terrorist?" I said.

"The wreckage eventually washed up on shore. They took every-thing to a hangar and put it together, piece by piece."

"Have you been there?" Bryce said.

Sam nodded.

"Did you see where your wife was sitting—and Dad?"

Again he nodded. "Felt like a graveyard. There were two huge holes in the fuselage—one below, one above. The investigators always assumed a missile made the hole. And with a terrorist taking credit for it, it seemed like a done deal.

"But they found a piece of those two holes—at least that's what they think it is. That piece and another under the plane where the fuel tank is made them investigate again. Now they think the middle fuel tank might have ignited and blown up."

"What do *you* think?"

Sam paused. "In my gut I know it was bin Asawe. I could be wrong, I guess. I've been wrong before."

"What was it like for the passengers?" Bryce said.

Sam leaned forward. "The cockpit and first-class cabin broke off and fell first. The engines would have kept pushing the rest of the plane up, which meant it would have been almost impossible to breathe." He rubbed his hands together. "Then the rest of the plane, with your dad and my wife and daughter, turned and fell."

I closed my eyes. I had hoped it happened in an instant, that everyone had died fast and felt nothing. That's still what I want to believe.

"Every day I think about them," Sam continued. "And every day I want to get that—" he stopped, and I think he wanted to say a bad word—"that man. And I feel like that's one thing God has for me to do before I die."

It was the first time I could remember Sam bringing up God on his own.

I had wondered if my dad had had time to think about us before he died. Did he call out Mom's name? Did he try to write a note? Did he pray? try to help the people around him?

CHAPTER 38

☺ *Bryce* ☺

Leigh drove us to the courts. Randy was going in to work late, so he would give Guy's car the once-over. I could tell Leigh was excited about the car because she asked questions about the camp, if we had much competition, that kind of thing. I couldn't imagine she really cared. She had no idea we had just talked to her dad about the plane crash.

We got there early and waited in the parking lot. Guy rumbled in and handed the keys to the clunker to Leigh.

When she was gone, Ashley and I did our stretches like good little campers, then took the first court and started hitting. Ashley's strokes were getting better. She hit with more authority, and when I came to the net, she zinged a forehand that stunned me. I barely got it back over.

The rest of the campers straggled in and filled the courts. Guy brought his usual load of tennis balls and had one of his high school assistants take attendance.

Golfers are always at the club early in the summer, but it takes a while for office people and others to arrive. We were in a heated round of knock-out, a little different than king of the court, when the cashier from the pro shop ran from the side entrance to the indoor tennis center. I was trying to concentrate on competing with Maddox, but when a Red Rock police car pulled up, I looked away, and Maddox hit a backhand past me and grinned.

Guy's pager went off, and he told everyone to take a break. Then he headed to the club.

"Think this is about last night?" Ashley said, as Mr. Grassel puttered quickly toward the country club in his cart.

"Either that or Leigh found out Guy's car doesn't have an engine."

CHAPTER 39

✱ Ashley ✱

An officer came over the hill with Guy and the cashier, whose face looked as tight as the strings on Maddox's racket.

The officer asked us to step away from the bench where our tennis bags sat. I know there are rules about searching people's things, but I didn't have anything to hide, and nobody else seemed upset about it.

The officer went right to Bryce's tennis bag and unzipped it. Bryce made a funny face at me, then turned around as the officer pulled the sides back. He looked straight at Bryce. "Is this yours?"

Bryce nodded, and I felt a sinking feeling in my stomach.

The officer reached in and pulled out a green money bag. Everybody gasped.

"Oh no," Bryce muttered.

"Follow me, son," the officer said.

Guy told me to stay, but there was no way I was going to let Bryce face this alone. "Somebody planted that!" I said.

Mr. Grassel joined the group as we walked toward the squad car. The cashier was on his cell phone, telling someone the bag had been recovered. He looked through the contents. "All the checks are here, but there's a few hundred dollars in cash missing."

Guy took me by the arm. "You're staying here."

CHAPTER 40

☺ *Bryce* ☺

The first person I thought about was Sean, the high school kid who had said he had a plan to make some money. I hadn't seen him around the courts that morning, but it was possible he had slipped the thing into my bag. But how could he have gotten into the safe? And who would have known which bag was mine?

I felt like a criminal again, especially when they called our house. I knew Sam was gone, and Mom didn't answer. The officer asked for her cell-phone number, but she didn't answer that either.

"You can't think I'm dumb enough to report the break-in last night and then keep the money in my bag," I said. I could feel my face turning redder than Rudolph's nose.

"How did you know there was a break-in?"

I told him about coming back for Ashley's bag and what had happened. "We called Mr. Grassel, and he came and locked the place down."

The officer looked like this was news to him.

I had to ask. "How did you know to look in my bag?"

"Someone phoned in an anonymous tip. Said it was one of the kids at the tennis camp."

We walked inside the country-club offices, a place I was becoming familiar with. I thought about asking for a lawyer, but Jill Davidson walked in and sat beside me. "You poor thing. They think you did this?"

She lit into the officer. "It's clear this young man is innocent. Why would he report the building being open and then hide the money in such an obvious place? It doesn't make sense."

"He could have hidden the money outside and picked it up this morning," the cashier said.

"Then where's the cash? And how did he get the combination to the safe? And how did he get into the building? And once he got in, why did he call us? His sister would have to be lying too. It's clear he's been set up."

"I'm just trying to find out what happened, ma'am," the officer said. He turned to me. "You want to tell us where you put the cash?"

"I didn't do this. You could check for fingerprints. I've never touched that bag."

"You could have used gloves," the cashier said.

Jill rolled her eyes. "Oh, come on. This is ridiculous."

The officer took off his cap and scratched his head. "You have anybody here who doesn't like you? who has it in for you?"

I couldn't think of anyone but Duncan, and he wouldn't do this.

"I heard a high school kid talking about having a plan about making some money," I said.

I told him about Sean, and the officer took notes. I was beginning to think I was part of something even bigger than my being accused of stealing, but I couldn't figure it out. It made me feel better knowing I was innocent and that Jesus had been falsely accused, but I was mad enough to spit.

CHAPTER 41

✾ Ashley ✾

I tried to do the drills, but I kept looking at the country club, wondering what was happening. Hayley asked if I was all right. I shook my head and felt like I was going to cry.

"It's gonna be okay," she said.

We broke for lunch and I ran to the office. The police officer's squad car was still there. Not much happens in Red Rock. Besides the stuff Bryce and I have uncovered, the biggest theft was someone stealing from Burger Barn two years ago. (It turned out that the thief had planned the thing with one of the guys who worked in the drive-thru.)

Bryce was coming down the stairs as I walked in. "What happened?" I said.

He told me how he'd gone round and round with the officer. "I guess they doubt I'm the thief. They're supposed to interview the high school helpers this afternoon."

"That Sean kid too?"

Bryce nodded.

The officer asked my side of the story. It must have jibed with Bryce's, because he excused me. The afternoon session was canceled, I guess, because a lot of the kids used their cell phones to call home. Some—mostly the ones tired of doing drills—said they weren't coming back.

Whoever was trying to shut down the country club was doing a good job.

CHAPTER 42

◑ *Bryce* ◑

I called Leigh at the auto shop. Randy had looked at the car and suggested she get a pro to check the engine. "I know the brakes are bad," she said, "and Randy says the transmission feels funny."

Leigh said she'd come get us within the hour.

We walked Hayley home, and she seemed a little distracted.

Finally, she turned. "Look, you guys are my friends, but my dad is having a real problem with all the stuff going on. Maybe it's better if you don't come to my house."

"What are you talking about?" Ashley said.

"It's okay," I said. "I'll wait at the club until Leigh comes."

"It's not just you," Hayley said, looking shyly at Ashley.

Ashley turned away. "Fine. See you tomorrow."

"There goes another friend," I said as we walked back to the club.

"Her dad can't honestly believe you had anything to do with this."

I shrugged. "He must. I just can't figure why anyone would try to kill the country club. What good would that do? Maybe it's someone who doesn't like golf, swimming, and tennis. Makes them mad just hearing *ping*, *splash*, and *thwop*."

That made Ashley smile. We waited in the parking lot—sweat pouring—for a half hour. We found some shade and studied people coming and going. The pine trees smelled funny and oozed resin.

Leigh pulled up, and Guy bounded out of the club with something in his hand.

We hurried over as Leigh was explaining that the mechanics had found "leaking oil, the transmission's almost gone, and the brakes are in bad shape."

"So you're not interested?" Guy said, his jaw set. "I have the title and everything. I have other people looking at it. I just thought it would be a good school car for you. Has a lot of miles left in it."

"Believe me, I want a car more than anything," Leigh said.

"Plus, I'm probably not going to be here that much longer."

Leigh held up a hand. "I paid the mechanic 45 bucks of my own money hoping my boyfriend was wrong. It would have helped if you'd have told me about any problems before I had it checked out."

The two stared at each other.

I said, "Why aren't you going to be around much longer?"

Guy glanced at me. "You should know. All the stuff going on around here. People are leaving the club at a record pace. Asking for their money back. Won't be long until they ask me to leave."

I looked at the title. The name under Vehicle Owner was Wesley

Collins from Castle Rock. I wanted to ask him who that was, but the longer Leigh took, the more Guy furrowed his brow.

He folded the title. "I didn't know there was anything wrong with it. It runs fine. Let me know if you change your mind."

CHAPTER 43

✖ Ashley ✖

Leigh drove us home, sighing and shaking her head. I said I thought she had made a good decision, but that didn't seem to help.

I felt like I'd lost a friend when Hayley turned away from us. I guess I could understand her parents being suspicious of us, but Hayley had to know better. It made me want to solve this mystery fast so things could get back to normal.

Leigh went straight to her room, and Bryce ran for the computer. He typed *Wesley Collins* and *Castle Rock* into a search for phone numbers, but it didn't bring up any matches.

He said, "Something about Guy makes me nervous, but I can't put my finger on it."

"It's not a crime to sell a broken-down car."

"But why would there be another name on the title?"

I shrugged. "Maybe he never got it changed after he bought it." I sat beside him and stared at the computer. "What if this country-club thing is not about putting people out of work? Maybe there's something we're not seeing."

I took the keyboard and did a search on Red Rock Country Club. I went to the newspaper archives and finally came upon a news story with a photo of several people sitting around a big oak table. The caption read, "Local developer makes offer to Red Rock Country Club board."

As I scrolled through the story, Bryce scooted closer.

Harold Ashworth's name is known throughout Red Rock and the surrounding area for building lavish houses. Lots of them. Close together.

Perhaps that's why the board of troubled Red Rock Country Club rejected an offer from the builder to buy the country-club property. One member of the board, who asked to remain anonymous, says he doesn't want fairways turned into driveways.

"Ashworth is a vulture," the anonymous member said. "He knows we're in bad shape, and he wants to gobble up our property so he can make a lot of money and move on to the next development."

Ashworth says he doesn't appreciate being called a vulture and that his motives are pure. "I've been a member here since we moved to the area, and I don't want to see it go under either. But if our area can't support a country club, I'd like to turn it into a nice community."

"Ashworth," Bryce said. "That's got to be Mad Dog Maddox's dad."

CHAPTER 44

◑ *Bryce* ◑

The police released my **ATV** Saturday morning, and I rode near the red rocks behind our house. It's peaceful back there, and I took a pad of paper to think about my dad. I jotted down a few things I wanted to say at our memorial service and headed back to the house.

Ashley and I rode to Maddox's place, not that far from the country club. We parked at the end of the brick driveway by the manicured lawn.

The house looked like it belonged on a magazine cover—*Beautiful Homes* or something like that. I thought any minute big Dobermans would run out and bark at us, but we made it all the way to the front porch before anything barked, and it was just a little yippy dog that's hair was so long it couldn't see a thing. I guess it smelled us.

We rang the doorbell, and when Maddox opened the door a blast of cold air hit us. It felt like we were walking into a freezer instead of his living room.

His partner, Tiffany, was right behind him, and she smiled at us like a mountain lion getting ready for a kill.

"Thirsty?" Maddox said.

He led us to the kitchen and opened a fridge that contained every kind of iced tea invented. We chose a couple and followed him as he pointed out different rooms in the house. "I'll give you more of a tour after we play."

His little sister splashed in the pool outside, and Maddox yelled at her not to get water on us.

Mrs. Ashworth stood. She was tall, very tan, and had blonde hair. She wore sunglasses and lots of lipstick and held a new paperback in one hand and a bottle of tea in the other. "So you're the Timberlines," she said. "Maddox tells me you're pretty good players."

Was that all he had told her?

"Bryce is a lot better than I am," Ashley said.

We headed to the court, past the splashing, giggling girl and her inflatable ladybug. The court, unseen from the house, lay behind a row of pine trees. A tall fence circled it, and I couldn't believe what was attached to the top. A thick mesh material almost like a tent ran around the entire court, blocking the sun.

"Almost like playing indoors," I said.

"Yeah, it's all right," Maddox said. He fired up a gas-powered leaf blower and chased pine needles away.

We warmed up, and I could tell by the way Tiffany grunted when she hit her ground strokes that this was going to be serious.

CHAPTER 45

✖ Ashley ✖

It was hard to concentrate with so many things going on—the stuff at the club, the anniversary of Dad's death, the clues that might lie in Maddox's house. As Maddox spun his racket to see who would serve first, I wondered if he was involved with the vandalism. He was close enough to spread the grass killer, and he could have even been the midnight jogger.

Maddox served first. I played the deuce court, and his first serve whizzed past me like a bullet.

Bryce banged his hand on the strings and nodded. "It's okay."

Bryce got the next serve back, but just barely, and Tiffany moved in for the kill. I had seen Maddox and Tiffany play a couple of other teams, but I didn't know they were this good.

There's a mental game with sports that I don't like. As soon as you walk onto a court, people compare themselves with you, wondering whether they can beat you. I felt it the first day at the camp. I even heard someone whisper, "She's not that good" when I made a bad shot. And a lot of the competition is mental. If you get down on yourself and start thinking you're terrible, you'll play that way.

Maddox showed confidence. Lots of it. He moved like he'd been born with a tennis racket in his hand, which would have been pretty painful for his mom when you think about it. I couldn't help comparing myself to Tiffany. She wasn't as good as Maddox, and I figured their strategy was to scare us with his serve, attempt to blow us out in the first game, try hard to break Bryce's serve, and roll to victory. I really didn't care, but I could tell Bryce was into it.

We got one point when Tiffany missed an overhead and put it into the net. Otherwise, Maddox was in control. We switched sides and Bryce took the balls. You have to have a lot of confidence in your brother not to hit you when you move to the net and turn your back to him. I took my position and watched Tiffany's eyes as Bryce hit a nice topspin serve to her backhand. I anticipated it perfectly, intercepted her shot, and put it away to the left, into the fence.

"Nice shot," Maddox said with a wink. I didn't know whether he really meant it.

"You should have moved on that one," someone said. It was an older man with glasses. I recognized Mr. Ashworth from the newspaper article.

Maddox's reaction was immediate. His shoulders slumped, his arm went limp, the racket top clacked against the court, and he lowered his head.

"All those lessons haven't taught you a thing, have they, Son?"

Bryce had run for the ball and passed me heading for the baseline. "Must not have seen the first game," he whispered.

"Hi, Mr. Ashworth," I said. "I'm Ashley."

He nodded, then shot a stare at his son. "Move your feet. You're impersonating a statue."

Maddox moved into position, hopping from one foot to the other and twirling his racket. Tiffany stared ahead like a robot. I figured she'd seen this before.

Bryce took a long time serving, and when he hit it, it didn't sound like his usual first serve. He had taken something off it—whether to let Maddox hit it or mess up his timing, I didn't know—but the effect was dramatic. Maddox wound up but got way out in front of the ball and hit it wide to my right.

"Don't overswing!" his dad yelled. "What are you thinking? You're trying too hard."

Maddox dropped his head and trudged toward the net.

His dad waved at the court and walked to the house.

I smiled. "Is he always that encouraging?"

Maddox didn't smile. He pursed his lips and hopped.

Bryce won his serve. Then we broke Tiffany's serve for a 2–1 lead. On the third point of the next game, I hit my first serve into the net, and the ball rolled to the right. I hit my second serve, and Tiffany returned it to my feet. I made a pretty good pickup and kept it away from Maddox. Tiffany got to it and hit a lob to my right. I moved back toward the sideline, then felt a sharp pain in my ankle.

I went down hard.

CHAPTER 46

☺ *Bryce* ☺

Maddox tried to warn Ashley before she stepped on the ball.
I should have picked it up, but it had rolled to the right and I thought
it would stay there.

Ashley lay on the court holding her ankle. She wasn't crying, but
I could tell she was close. It was clear she wasn't going to get up
and walk it off.

"I'll get some ice," Tiffany said, hurrying off.

"Did it snap?" I said, slipping her shoe off. Her ankle was already
swollen.

Ashley shook her head. "I just rolled it, I think."

Ashley wouldn't let us carry her. We pulled her up and she hopped,
wincing. I grabbed her left arm and draped it over my shoulder, and
Maddox took her right arm.

"No hurry," I said.

"I know what you're trying to do," Maddox said, smiling. "Fake an injury so you can win the tournament at the end of camp."

Mr. Ashworth's home office had an entrance on the ground level, so it was easy to help Ashley inside.

"Put her on the chaise," Maddox said.

A chaise is a humongous leather chair. It was long and seemed like a perfect place to nap.

Tiffany brought ice in a plastic freezer bag and was followed by Maddox's mother. Tiffany placed the ice on Ashley's ankle and stood back like she'd just saved her life.

I thought Sam's office in the barn was nice, but it was a dump compared with this. Building awards and pictures of houses decorated the walls. I noticed a golf ball encased in glass, and Maddox said that was his dad's hole-in-one ball at some place named Pebble Beach. I would have loved to be left here for an hour to look through his files, but we were lucky to even be inside.

"No computer?" I said.

Maddox motioned to the far wall and a huge plasma screen. He pulled a keyboard tray out from the desk and punched a key. The screen, almost as big as the wall, came to life.

The screen showed icons for his e-mail, word processing, and home design. One looked like a map, but Maddox clicked on the design button and showed us something his dad was building that looked bigger than the Pepsi Center—that's where the Nuggets and Avalanche play in Denver.

"I'll get a bandage," Mrs. Ashworth said. Tiffany followed her to the house.

"I'll grab your stuff from the court," Maddox said.

CHAPTER 47

✖ Ashley ✖

Bryce stared at the computer screen, grabbed the cordless mouse, and moved the arrow.

"What are you doing?" I whispered.

He minimized the design program. "Looking for something."

He clicked on a little map in the corner, and it blew up to gigantic size. It was a map of Red Rock and the surrounding area that looked like it had the measles because there were red dots all over it. Bryce put the mouse over one of the dots and double clicked. Up popped a listing of houses, names of owners, street numbers, and an inset picture of each house.

"This guy sure builds a lot of stuff," I said.

Bryce went back to the main map and several yellow arrows.

"What are those?" I said.

He double clicked on one near the Briargate area and up popped names, addresses, phone numbers, but no actual buildings. *Pending* was written across the top.

"Looks like where he plans to build," Bryce said.

"There's one in Red Rock," I said.

Bryce clicked on it. There was only one address, the Red Rock Country Club.

"What's that mean?" I said.

"It means you're snooping where you shouldn't be," someone said.

CHAPTER 48

⊙ *Bryce* ⊙

I almost jumped out of my skin. Mr. Ashworth stood in the doorway, staring at us like we had just double-faulted on match point. He had thinning hair and his middle was round. He had an angular, birdlike face, like he could peck your eyes out. It was like looking into the ocean, his eyes were so blue.

I imagined him bossing his workers and yelling at contractors, but as hard as I tried I couldn't see him playing with his kids or their toys.

He held up a towel. "I heard you were hurt, young lady."

Ashley nodded and looked at her ankle. I looked at her ankle. Her ankle was becoming a lot more interesting now that the guy who owned the office was in the room. I couldn't stop staring at her ankle.

"She really twisted it," I said.

To my surprise, he didn't kick us out or yell at us or even mention the snooping again. He slipped the towel under Ashley's foot. He had to know the ice would melt and the water would stain his expensive leather chaise. But he didn't seem to care. He just lifted her ankle and pressed it a couple of places.

She winced.

"That hurt?"

"A little."

"Keep ice on it—20 minutes on, 20 minutes off—until tomorrow. You'll probably be back on the court next week."

I wanted to exit the computer program and apologize, but before I could say anything he moved to the door. "I'll drive your sister home. We'll keep her ATV until you can pick it up."

I helped Ashley to his truck. Maddox put our stuff in the back and waved as they pulled out.

"Guess we'll have to finish this on the country-club courts," Maddox said.

One of the garage doors was open, and what I saw inside stopped me in my tracks. An open bag of grass killer.

"Forget something?" Maddox said. He flicked a button, and the door silently closed.

"Just heading home," I said.

CHAPTER 49

Ashley

Mr. Ashworth drove past the country club and over the hill toward our house in silence.

"So, you're a builder," I said. I looked out the window and rolled my eyes. Was there any good way to start a conversation with this guy?

"Yeah, the very first one I built is coming up," he said, pointing. It was a small house with a shake-shingle roof. "I was always handy with tools when I was a kid. I built stuff in my dad's garage. Tinkered in shop class. Never thought I'd be doing this."

"What happened?"

"My dad died just before I was supposed to leave for college. My mom and younger sister were alone with no one to care for them. I put college off and started working for a guy my dad knew, a carpenter. He taught me about building."

Mr. Ashworth didn't seem the type to open up and give his life story. But here he was, spilling it in the front seat of his truck.

"I moved from Kansas because houses were booming then. Went to work for a small company and scraped together enough money for a down payment on some land here in Red Rock. Bought that little piece back there for a few thousand dollars, worked on the house at night after work, and moved my mom and sister here.

"I sold it and used the money to build a bigger house. Pretty soon I was working on two, selling them for twice what I'd put into them, and I was on my own. That's when I met my wife. Maddox came along a couple of years later."

"How many houses have you built?"

He shrugged. "My company has built thousands."

"Any in our neighborhood?"

He smiled. "A few. Didn't build yours. That was a friend of mine."

He turned the air conditioner up, and I scooted forward. My ankle throbbed, and I tried to keep the ice on it as we went around a curve.

I took a deep breath. "I saw an article in the paper from a few months ago. It said you were trying to buy the country club. Are you going to build houses there?"

The corners of his mouth turned up. "The yellow arrows you and your brother saw are simply my way of dreaming. Sure, I'd like to build in that area. I have ever since I first heard of the Bascom place."

The name rang a bell, but I couldn't remember where I had heard it. "Bascom?"

"John Bascom was an old prospector. His house was somewhere around here—no one is sure where. Some think it sat where the country club is now. He owned the land they used for the golf course and pool and tennis courts. I tried to buy it a long time ago, but the deal fell through and the country club got it, which was fine. But now that they're having problems, I'd like to see my dream realized."

He turned into our driveway, parked, and turned to me. "Miss Timberline, you and your brother are snooping around people's private property. I suggest you stick to something you're good at. Like tennis."

His words stung.

"Why are you so mean to Maddox?" I said quickly.

The question seemed to stop him. He put his hand on the steering wheel and set his jaw. "I motivate my son to be a better player. That's between him and me and has nothing to do with you."

CHAPTER 50

◔ *Bryce* ◔

When I got home Ashley told me what Mr. Ashworth had said. I told her what I had seen in the garage. "What if he put Maddox up to the vandalism? Did you see how Maddox reacted to his yelling?"

She nodded. "So Maddox stole the money and framed you?"

"It'd be a good way to get us out of the competition. We have a good chance of beating him."

"But how would he get the combination?"

I sat on a stool next to her. "I've been thinking about what you said. You know, that this might be about something bigger. Mr. Ashworth wants the club to go under—that's for sure. And with his money and contacts he probably could have had somebody on the inside give him the combination."

Ashley pursed her lips. "I'm not sure Mr. Ashworth would do something that desperate. He's a jerk as a father, but if you heard his story—"

"Then what about the grass killer?" I said.

"If it's a crime to have grass killer in your garage, just about everybody in Red Rock should be in jail."

CHAPTER 51

Ashley

On the anniversary of Dad's plane crash I hobbled down to breakfast and put ice on my ankle. It felt stiffer than the day before but not as sore.

Since Sam and Mom were not going to the official memorial service, Bryce and I had asked if we could have our own at the Garden of the Gods.

Mom nodded. "He would have loved it there."

The Garden of the Gods has lots of rock formations similar to the red rocks behind our house. There are hiking trails, and locals and tourists come to rock climb or take pictures of Pikes Peak.

Leigh didn't want to go, but Sam talked her into it. I know she was upset about the car. The start of her senior year was getting closer, and I think she was afraid she'd have to ride the bus.

We piled in the car and got Dylan squared away in his car seat.

"We're going to a memorial service," Mom said.

"What's a bumorial service?"

"Memorial," I said. "It's where you remember people who are special to you who have died."

He thought a moment. "Who are we bemembering?"

"Sam's our dad now," I said, "but before that we had another dad."

"In the picture," Dylan said, excited. He has a photo of Dad holding him in his baby blanket.

"Right. That's who we're remembering. And Leigh is remembering her mom and sister."

We got on I-25 and headed south, Dylan deep in thought. He seemed distracted by the planes and parachutes at the Air Force Academy. Then he turned to Bryce. "What does *dead* mean?"

CHAPTER 52

☺ *Bryce* ☺

Sam looked at me in the rearview mirror. I wondered if what I said next would make it into one of Mom's books someday.

"Remember my sugar glider?" I said. A sugar glider is like a flying squirrel, small and furry with big eyes. It made a weird noise, and I had to wear gloves when I got it out of its cage.

"Princess!" Dylan said.

"Right. Well, remember the day Princess stopped moving?"

Dylan nodded. He had good reason to remember because he's the one who had put my gloves on, stuck his hand in the cage, and played with Princess when he wasn't supposed to. I can only imagine the last few minutes of Princess's life, but at three, Dylan had no idea what he was doing. I found Princess on the floor of my room, cold and stiff.

"When a pet or a person stops breathing and their heart stops beating, they die. That's what dead means."

Dylan looked out the window at a truck. Finally he turned back. "Did they wrap our dad in a paper towel like Princess?"

"No, but they buried him in a big box called a casket." I didn't want to tell Dylan that when a plane crashes you don't find whole bodies. "That was a long time ago."

"I hurt Princess," Dylan said.

"I know. It's okay."

"Why did Daddy die?"

I tried to get inside Dylan's little mind. I didn't want him to think someone had put on a big glove and squeezed our dad too tight. "Bad people made his plane crash." I caught Sam's eye in the mirror.

"Oh," Dylan said. "Are the bad people going to hurt us?"

"Won't let them," I said. "If they try, we'll punch them in the nose."

That made Dylan laugh like a hyena.

Deep down I wasn't so sure about the bad people. Sam had a look that said he would protect us, but I don't know if there's anyone who can keep the bad people from hurting us except God, and sometimes I even wonder about him.

I thought about asking Mom why we couldn't go to the real memorial service, but I figured that would bring up more questions from Dylan.

CHAPTER 53

❀ Ashley ❀

There weren't many people in the park, just a few joggers and people walking their dogs.

Leigh took Dylan's hand and walked ahead of us down a path. A couple rode by on bicycles. Sam pointed out a pair of prairie falcons in the cleft of a rock overhead.

I didn't want to walk far on my ankle, so we found a place close to the parking lot that Bryce and I had thought about, a little circle with benches all around. Rock walls loomed nearby, and it felt secluded.

Mom and Sam sat together. Leigh held Dylan on her lap. All of a sudden I felt nervous, like we were supposed to perform. Then I thought of Dad and why we were here.

Bryce pulled out a crumpled piece of paper and walked to the center of the circle. It probably seems to most people that Bryce only thinks about video games and sports, but I know better.

"It was about this time of day that the plane took off," he began. "Dad was in row 15. Leigh, your mom and sister were in row 14."

I couldn't look at Leigh. I stared at Bryce.

"Dad, I imagine where you are now is a lot nicer, but you would have liked this place. And you'd like Sam too. And Leigh. You guys would have had a lot of fun together.

"We're doing this not for you, but for us. To remember what you were like. To keep you alive in our hearts somehow. Every year that passes makes it seem a little less real. But today we remember you. And Sam's wife and daughter. And all the people on that plane. And we want you to know we love you and miss you." Bryce sat.

I stood and pulled out my own paper. "Dad, I think about the times you'd wake us up in the morning before school. The smell of your aftershave. The way you'd just sit there until I opened my eyes, and how you'd push the hair out of my face. I'll never forget the Santa pants you wore every Christmas. Your special blueberry pancakes you made us on Saturdays. I didn't realize how much I loved you back then, but I do now.

"I also remember how you answered questions about God. You didn't force stuff on us, but I can see now how much you believed and how much you wanted us to believe."

I'd been over this a hundred times so I wouldn't get choked up, but still my notes got blurry and my chin quivered.

"I know being separated from you is only temporary, though. The Bible says, 'Nothing can ever separate us from God's love. Neither death nor life, neither angels nor demons, neither our fears for today nor our worries about tomorrow—not even the powers of hell can separate us from God's love. No power in the sky above or in the earth below—indeed, nothing in all creation will ever be able to separate us from the love of God that is revealed in Christ Jesus our Lord.'

"I look forward to seeing you again, Dad. Today we remember you and say we love you."

CHAPTER 54

☺ *Bryce* ☺

Mom hadn't said anything about wanting to speak, but after she helped Ashley limp to the bench, she turned and cleared her throat.

"It's good to remember. And it's easy to be thankful for good memories. For picnics and twins and summer vacations at the beach. But it's also good to remember the hard times—the arguments over little things and the way you always came back to me. Loved me. You made me a better wife. A better wife to the husband I have now. And I know how much you prayed for me in those last months. Thank you for that."

Sam lumbered to the middle, shoved his hands into his pockets as far as they would go, and pulled his shoulders high. His voice was low and gravelly when he started, and I couldn't hear.

Then he cleared his throat and started again. "Lynn, I had no idea what I was in for when I married you. I thought we'd travel the world together. Thought we'd wind up on some island somewhere living in a hut. But things didn't work out that way. And when Leigh came along, I could see it in your eyes. Motherhood changed every-thing about you, and it was good. Your choices were good.

"Kayla, I wish I could have seen you grow up. I wish I'd had more time to take you places and do things with you. The zoo. Parades. I have a lot of regrets, but I cherish the memories.

"So today we remember you. The love we shared. We miss you."

I'd never heard Sam talk that way about his wife and daughter.

The biggest surprise came when Leigh held Dylan against her shoulder and stood. "Mom," she said, "I've been really angry the past few years because you left us. I know it wasn't your fault. I've always known that, but I'm still upset. Hurt. Maybe it's not you I'm angry at.

"We have a new family, and I'm thankful for it even though it's not perfect. I don't know if you ever pictured me buying a car. I don't know if you thought about me dating, but I guess you had to. I sure don't think you pictured me with a little brother like this guy." She hugged Dylan tight, and he looked at the sky like he was trying to see Dad or Leigh's mom. "Like Ashley and Bryce said, I miss you. And today I remember you."

Then Leigh's voice cracked. "And, Kayla, I wasn't always very nice to you, but I loved you a lot. I hope you know that."

Mom went to Leigh and hugged her. The two of them just stood and cried.

I took Dylan from Leigh's arms, and he said, "What's wrong?"

"It's okay, buddy. Sometimes remembering's hard."

I looked at the rocks behind us. The falcon had left its perch and soared overhead, its shadow passing. I wanted to join it and fly away. I didn't want to think about people dying and hear crying anymore. But I guess that's life.

Dylan seemed to believe that too because as we walked back to the car he said, "I'm hungry."

CHAPTER 55

✖ Ashley ✖

When I think of summer, I think of a song on the radio. Every year there's one that Bryce and I latch onto and wear out. This year it's a new Christian group singing about heaven—I couldn't help listening to it over and over. I bought it and burned a CD with the song 16 times in a row.

I told Bryce I was going to give my ankle one more day's rest, so I slept in Monday morning, and when I finally woke up I put the CD on. My ankle felt so much better that I almost asked Mom to drive me to the tennis camp, but instead I grabbed a bagel from the kitchen and a book from my shelf and curled up in bed. I opened my window and let the wind blow through.

Something had happened to our family at the memorial service. I knew Leigh wasn't going to change overnight and start treating us like real humans, but hearing her talk during the service and then seeing her laugh at lunch had given me a little hope.

The book wasn't doing it for me—maybe because the song I liked was on its 14th time through. I grabbed a notepad and wrote down as many clues about the country club as I could. Maddox's father was our main suspect, and Maddox could have been involved too.

Something Maddox's father had said came back as I wrote. The name *John Bascom* sounded familiar, but where had I heard it? I went downstairs to the computer as Mom headed out the door to take Dylan to a friend's to play.

I called up my favorite search engine, typing in the prospector's name. I found a picture of an old guy with a shovel on his shoulder standing next to a mule. The story said he came to Colorado in the 1800s and struck gold. One picture showed Bascom's family, including a little girl in a long dress. The article said the girl died in a flu epidemic.

Finally the name clicked. A few weeks before, Bryce and I had walked through an old haunted house overlooking our town. We found a secret entrance, and there were holes in the walls. Bryce's friend Jeff said people thought Bascom had hidden gold in there. It looked to us like the whole place had been searched so much that the house was ready to fall apart.

I studied Bascom's picture. *What secrets do you have?*

CHAPTER 56

☺ *Bryce* ☺

A couple of girls at camp asked where Ashley was.
Maddox and Tiffany asked not how she felt or if her ankle was
better but whether I thought she would be able to play Saturday.
I told them I was sure she would, that she was a real competitor,
and that we were going to wipe the court with them. (Okay, I said
everything but that last part.)

Maddox had wet hair, and I asked if he needed me to buy him
a hair dryer.

He smiled and leaned close. "Took a dip in the country-club pool.
Great way to wake up."

Guy arrived a few minutes late and seemed in a bad mood. He started us off with suicides, which I thought was curious for a Monday morning. If I ever become a tennis pro and get to run my own camp, I'll do it differently.

A few high school guys were talking during one of the new drills. I heard the name *Sean* and moved closer.

"Cops say someone said he'd told us he had a plan to make money," the guy said.

"How could they have known that?" another said.

"Everybody swears they didn't say anything to the cops," a skinny guy with a long neck said. Then he looked at me. "Hey, you were eating your lunch near us that day, weren't you?"

I looked behind me, then back at them. "Me?"

He moved toward me, banging his racket against a hand. He had big muscles for a skinny guy. His Adam's apple was as pointy as a canary's beak. It moved up and down as he swallowed. Funny what you notice when your life is about to end.

"Yeah," another guy said. "Him and his low-rent sister. They were there the whole time. I'll bet you tried to blame it on Sean."

I held up a hand. "Look, I told the police what I heard Sean say, but I didn't say he—"

"Sure you didn't," Adam's Apple interrupted. "You just put them on his trail to get them off yours."

Now they both moved toward me.

I decided to go on the offensive instead of backing away. "How do you guys know it wasn't Sean? Maybe he broke into the tennis center. Your friend could be the reason the club's going under."

The two looked at each other and rolled their eyes.

"How do you know his little moneymaking scheme wasn't a heist here?" I said.

Adam's Apple snickered. "Sean's scheme wasn't a country-club heist. He wants to start a lawn-watering business."

"Lawn watering?"

"Yeah, he said there were lots of people who didn't have sprinkler systems, and with the dry weather their grass died. He rode his bike up and down the road telling people he'd hook a hose up to their spigots and water their lawn every day."

"He was going to call it the Human Sprinkler," another guy said. "Ten bucks an hour and your lawn was guaranteed."

"Sean's not a very bright bulb, but we know him well enough to know he wouldn't steal or hurt the country club." They inched closer. "Now why would you sic the police on him?"

These guys seemed to think I was the real culprit, and they were going to knock a confession out of me with a couple of forehands to the knees.

But just then a whistle blew. The blessed whistle of Guy. What a lovely sound. When he ordered me to do 10 suicides, I knew he had to be the kindest man on the planet.

"This isn't over, kid," Adam's Apple said.

Rescued by suicides. How ironic.

CHAPTER 57

❊ Ashley ❊

My ankle felt uncomfortable as I rode my ATV to the country
club. I knew I couldn't park it there, but I could get close enough to
walk to the pool from the back side.

I'd called Marion Quidley and found out she was at the pool. I figured I'd find her, stick my foot in the hot tub, and get some answers.

I'd known Marion since the first day of school at Red Rock. She
wore thin glasses, the kind that make her look like a cat, and the
way she kept her hair and wore her clothes let you know she didn't
care what others thought. It was refreshing to watch her sneer at the
kids who had to have the best jeans or latest shoes.

One thing that makes Marion stand out in a crowd is her brain. She's one of the smartest kids in school, but she's also quirky. She believes there's a real Loch Ness Monster, crop circles are made by aliens trying to communicate with us, whales are smarter than we are, and other weird stuff.

The first thing she said after she found out my dad had been killed in the plane crash was that she thought the CIA was trying to frame terrorists and the whole thing was about an oil plot in the Middle East. It made me want to stay away from her—until I had problems in algebra, and then I decided I could put up with the wild theories.

I found Marion at the hot tub, soaking and reading *Rediscovering Your Inner Alien.*

I had my bathing suit on under my shorts, so I said hello and sat. It didn't take her long to launch into the book's main point, which was that we all have a little alien in us and we need to listen to that voice. I let her go on a few minutes, pretending to be interested.

Finally I steered the conversation to another subject. "Your mom's in the historical society, isn't she?"

Marion nodded. "Not much history around here, if you ask me. Now if you go to the Mayan ruins, you'll see an ancient civilization. Or the pyramids. And how did they get the know-how to build all that stuff? I think they had visitors from outer—"

"Has your mom ever said anything about an old house that used to be on this property?"

"The Bascom place?" I couldn't believe she knew the name that quickly. "Mom said it may have been built right over there." She gestured toward the tennis courts, at the very place where Bryce and I had seen upturned earth.

"What do you know about it?"

Marion scooted down a step in the hot tub and adjusted her

glasses. She told me stuff I'd mostly heard before with a few things she had added for spice. Mr. Bascom had made his fortune after speaking with some phantom on a hillside who pinpointed the gold, and after he became rich the phantom came back. That kind of stuff.

Then she said, "Mom said the documents they found recently had the plans for the old house and letters the guy had written that detailed the stuff he hid. It's probably the most interesting history I've heard around here. Other than the triple-murder trial they had back in—"

"Wait, they found documents? Where?"

"In the old vault at the country club. They switched over to a new safe recently, I guess so nobody would steal anything. A lot of good that did. And they found all these ratty pieces of paper and turned them over to the historical society."

"Who has them now?" I said.

Marion scratched her head. "My mom cataloged the papers and is going to turn them over to the society."

A whistle cut through the splashing and laughing in the pool. A lifeguard lifted a megaphone. He had muscular arms, a nice haircut, sunglasses, and a tan I would have paid for. "Everyone out of the pool and the hot tub! Now!"

When kids groaned and moved slowly, the guy clicked the megaphone again. "There are dangerous levels of chemicals. You'll have to get out now!"

Marion and I pulled our feet from the hot tub like it was filled with poisonous snakes. "How could the water change like that?" she said. "They check it before anyone goes in."

We stood around with everyone else while Mr. Pool (a guy in work clothes and carrying beakers) checked the chlorine levels.

Marion asked the lifeguard how the levels could be that out of whack. Sometimes girls ask a question like that because they just want to talk with some hunk, but Marion and I were really interested.

"I checked it before anybody got in," he said. "It was fine. Someone had to add chemicals since we opened."

Mr. Pool conferred with the lifeguard. Kids hopped on the hot concrete, waiting to go back in. Moms spread more suntan lotion on their kids' backs or stared at magazines. A couple of older women in swim caps seemed just as antsy to finish their laps as the kids did to get back in the pool.

"I'm sorry," the lifeguard said into the megaphone. "The pool is closed until further notice. We might be able to open tomorrow."

"Tomorrow?" several people said at once.

"We want our money back!" an older woman said.

"Yeah, we want a refund!" a woman said. "This is a joke."

"Great," I said to Marion. "More problems for the country club."

CHAPTER 58

☻ *Bryce* ☻

Ashley found me at lunch (which wasn't easy because I was hiding from the high schoolers) and told me what had happened at the pool. I told her what Maddox had said.

"What if he's the one who did it?" she said.

"Makes sense," I said. "He could have tossed the chemicals in after his swim and after their morning water test."

"You think his dad put him up to it?"

I shrugged. "All the clues point to it."

Ashley told me about the documents. "I'm going to drive to Marion's house and talk with her mom about them."

I told her about my talk with the two high schoolers. "Sure you don't want to come back and run suicides with me?"

"I'll pass this time. See you at home."

I headed to the empty courts, figuring I could hit against the green monster and score some points with Guy if he saw me practicing. Plus, it would be harder for the goons to whale on me in the open. I hoped.

I picked up my racket and noticed Maddox's tennis bag lying on a bench near the courts. You couldn't miss it because his was the expensive leather one.

I glanced around, then dropped a ball near the bag. When I picked it up, I peeked inside. Maddox had two new cans of balls, several rackets, some sweatbands, grip tape, and a bottle of Gatorade. I lifted the side pocket that held his wallet and watch.

I was about to walk away when something caught my eye. In one corner was a plastic tube with the stopper pulled out. The inside was empty, except for a few traces of powder.

"Looking for something?" Maddox said behind me.

I straightened up and dropped my racket. I picked it up, my hands shaking. "Want to hit some before we start?"

He gave me a wary look, then grinned as Tiffany walked up. "No thanks."

CHAPTER 59

✖ Ashley ✖

Marion's house looked like a double trailer. It sat on a slab of concrete, and someone had put up window boxes with flowers to make it look prettier.

I'd never heard anything about Mr. Quidley, so I looked closely at the pictures on the wall when I walked in. I'd heard many theories from kids at school about why Marion was the way she was. Sometimes you don't ask about someone's personal life because you're afraid of what you might find. In Marion's case I was curious and figured this was a good time to talk. I knew Marion wasn't a Christian. Some said she was an atheist, but I couldn't believe that because she had all these wild theories about evil things.

Marion's mom was a heavyset woman with dark hair and tight clothes. I could tell by the family pictures that she had been thin when she was younger. The living room looked like there might be ancient artifacts under the couch cushions. Newspapers lay scattered, magazines and empty cereal bowls sat on tables, and candy wrappers dotted the floor. Marion tried to clean up while I stood there, but it was like trying to lower the level of Lake Michigan by dipping a coffeepot in it.

Marion's mom cleared a place for me to sit. She smiled, if you could call it that, and I told her I wanted to know more about the papers from the country club.

"Interesting find," she said, lifting the lid to a piano bench. "We're lucky someone thought to give them to us rather than tossing them."

The phone rang and she let the lid fall. "Be right back."

Marion sat across from me wrapped in a towel. She studied my face like some difficult crossword puzzle.

"I like your view," I said, pointing out the back window at the Front Range.

She stared. Finally she said, "I know what you're thinking."

"What?" *I* didn't even know what I was thinking.

"You're thinking, *how* could we live in such a place as this?"

"What's wrong with it?"

She tilted her head and looked over her glasses. "I've seen your house. Never been inside, but I can imagine."

Marion was looking at me the same way I had looked at Maddox, and that made me uncomfortable. "Who cares what kind of house a person has?"

She snorted and looked toward the kitchen. I figured this was as good a time as any to ask about her dad. She gestured at an old picture on the wall. "That's what he looked like when he was just out of high school. Strong and lean. Wanted to play baseball. Mom said he was pretty good."

"What happened to him?"

She looked at the floor. "Want something to drink? Water? Maybe some lemonade?"

"Water would be great."

Marion's mom continued on the phone. I stood and looked at the picture of her father. Beside it was a photo of the three of them, her dad with an arm around his wife and the other balancing Marion on his shoulders. It reminded me of a picture of our real dad holding Bryce and me right after we were born.

I don't know what happened to the water, but Marion brought back three glasses of lemonade and handed me one. She put another on the coffee table and took the other to a back room.

"Here you go, Dad," she said.

"Thanks, honey," a voice said weakly.

CHAPTER 60

☻ *Bryce* ☻

Clouds rolled in and we moved indoors. Guy had the high schoolers run us through more drills before we played our matches. I figured I'd sit on the sidelines since Ashley wasn't around, but Guy paired me with Leslie Bolan. Her brother, Lou, had some kind of appointment.

I was torn about Maddox. Part of me wanted to go to the people at the pool and tell them what I suspected. Another part of me said wait. I had jumped to wrong conclusions before.

We took the court against a pair I hadn't played before. Leslie bounced and hopped trying to get loose. We won the toss, and she started in with hand signals behind her back.

I called her to the baseline. "Look, I don't do well with signals. You play the line and I'll take this side and we'll see what happens."

The look on her face was priceless, like it had never occurred to her that she had to do only one thing instead of 20. Sports are like that. Sometimes when you think too much you mess up. I think it's best to just play.

I served, and our opponent hit a sharp forehand straight at Leslie. I had done the same thing to her the week before, and she had locked up and barely hit the ball into the net. This time she got her racket out in front of her and hit the ball squarely in the middle so it made a *thwop*, and it bounced harmlessly to the curtain.

She turned and looked at me like she had just discovered the goose that lays golden tennis balls.

I gave her a thumbs-up. "Nice shot."

"Yeah," she said. She looked like she couldn't wait to hit the thing again.

I was about to serve when I noticed the high school guys bunched together near the pro shop, looking straight at me. Sean stood in the middle of them. His jaw was set and his eyes narrowed.

CHAPTER 61

❀ Ashley ❀

Marion invited me into her father's room. His face was sunken, and he looked nothing like the healthy guy in the picture. He said he had worked construction for years before an accident. They had lived in a nice section of town until he got hurt. Then they found this place. It had been three years since he had been able to work.

Marion looked at him like he was King Arthur. "It's hot in here," she said, turning the fan so it made the bedsheet flutter.

"Not too much air," he said, then turned to me. "You're the Timberline girl. I read about your brother in the paper."

"He's my twin," I said.

"Ashley and I have some classes together," Marion said, fluffing his pillow. He touched her arm. I thought about my own dad and wished he had only been hurt instead of killed.

"Marion's told me how smart you and your brother are," he said.

"Marion's the smart one," I said. "I have to study all night, and she comes in and aces tests without even cracking a book."

He gave a tired smile. "I'm hoping she'll get a scholarship."

"She deserves one," I said.

Her phone call over, Mrs. Quidley came and shooed us out. She led me to the kitchen, where she had cleaned off a three-foot section of the table, and put some old documents in front of me.

"I'm holding these until our next historical society meeting. I've cataloged the pages."

"Marion said something about a diagram of the house."

She flipped through the crackling pages. "Here you are."

I gasped. It was hard to see with all the lines and numbers around the building plans, but when I stepped back from the drawing and looked at the whole picture, the Bascom place looked like the haunted house we had seen with our friend Jeff. Had everyone mixed that house up with the real Bascom place?

Mrs. Quidley had stuck big Post-it notes on the pages, numbering them and jotting a brief description. I found a letter from the man's brother dated April 23, 1892 and was amazed at the perfect handwriting.

We hear through a mutual acquaintance that your work in Colorado has become profitable. Not all have seen your level of success, but we are happy for your fortune and trust that the rewards won't cloud your judgment. If what we hear is untrue and your fortunes are not as the rumors say, know

that we feel the same way as we always have and that you
have a place here with us if you desire it.

I'd never read anything like that letter and wondered what it
would have sounded like if Mr. Bascom and his brother had e-mailed
each other.

"Any mention of gold?" I said.

"The letters talk about his 'fortune,' but that's it," Mrs. Quidley
said. "Records at the society say he died in a mining accident, and
no one ever recovered any money or gold."

CHAPTER 62

☺ *Bryce* ☺

Leslie played a lot better than she had with Lou, and we won by a couple of games. She smiled as we walked off, as if she couldn't wait to tell someone.

I gave her a high five and hurried to get my stuff. She wanted to talk, but I was in a hurry. I ran behind the green curtain into the locker room. I expected Sean to jump out from a locker, but it didn't happen.

I walked into the lobby, and my heart skipped a beat when the high schoolers weren't there. I hit the door and ran the back way up the hill through the pine trees. It hadn't rained after all, but the skies still threatened.

Mom wasn't in the parking lot. *The one day she has to be late.*

I wanted to hide behind some cars, but people might think I was trying to steal something, so I moved back to the country club. Camp kids were leaving. Hayley cut through the empty driving range. I waved but she didn't see me.

I'd been waiting for Mom a few minutes when the group of high school guys, including Sean, showed up. Most of them were at least a head taller than me. So much for the growth spurt I'd prayed for.

Sean was the smallest and wiriest. "So you're the kid who sicced the police on me?"

Adam's Apple chuckled.

"Uh, I didn't exactly—"

Sean poked a bony finger into my chest. "You don't lie about me and get away with it."

I couldn't believe I was being attacked by the Human Sprinkler. I glanced at the parking lot, but our car was nowhere in sight. Not that I wanted my mother to bail me out or anything. Okay, yes I did.

I cleared my throat and squeaked.

That made them laugh.

"All I did was tell them what I'd heard—"

"All you did was get them to come to my house looking for me," Sean said. "You know what happens to people who get the cops to come looking for me?"

I wondered if they were the vandals after all. Had they covered for Sean with the sprinkler story, when they'd been the ones working on sabotaging the club? One of them could have gotten the combination to the safe and contaminated the pool.

I looked into Sean's eyes, hoping there was something human in there other than his irises. He looked past me, and I turned to see Jill Davidson.

"Something I can help you gentlemen with?" she said.

"No, ma'am," Adam's Apple said.

"Good. Bryce, I need to see you."

CHAPTER 63

✖ Ashley ✖

The documents from Mr. Bascom didn't look valuable, but I couldn't help thinking there had to be a clue here.

Mrs. Quidley left me alone with the pages. Marion was with her father. *At least I was able to solve one mystery,* I thought. *I know what happened to Marion's dad.*

I reread the letters word for word. I like word jumbles, so I thought there might be a hidden message. I read words backward, took the first letters of each sentence, did everything I could to break the Bascom Code and finally decided there was no code.

I was gathering the papers to give back to Mrs. Quidley when I noticed something strange in the drawing of the old Bascom house. It had a faded mark at the top of the page that was curled around the edges.

"Do you know what made this mark?" I said.

"The drawing was rolled up like a scroll with a piece of string tied around it. The thing was almost disintegrated, so I threw it away."

"And this was the only thing rolled up like that?"

She nodded. "Why?"

I spread the page and looked in all four corners. The upper-right corner was faded and had been eaten away, but I could make out the curly mark. "What does that look like to you?"

"Maybe a number?"

"Who rolls up just one sheet of paper and ties it?" I said. "That looks like the bottom of a *3* to me. If it is, two pages are missing."

She studied the mark. "What are you getting at, Ashley?"

"There might have been something on those pages someone wants to keep hidden."

CHAPTER 64

◔ *Bryce* ◔

"What was going on out there?" Jill Davidson said as we sat in her office.

I gave her the short version, and she shook her head. "I can't believe they think you were involved." Her secretary brought her a phone message. "Thank you, Delores."

"Somebody's trying to shut you guys down," I said. "The only thing they haven't tried is setting a fire in the kitchen. Thanks for bailing me out."

"Those guys looked like they were up to no good," she said.

"Didn't get arrested today?" Mom said with a wink when I slid into the car.

"Is Bryce going to jail?" Dylan said.

Mom chuckled.

"Not if I can help it," I said.

Ashley was waiting for me at home, and the way she limped when I followed her upstairs made me think it would be at least another day before she was back on the court. And who knew how long before she was 100 percent.

She explained what she'd found at Marion's house—the historical documents, the missing pages, and the drawings of the Bascom house.

Ashley could tell by the way I screwed my face up that I thought this was a rabbit trail. "It may have nothing to do with the vandalism," she said, "but maybe it points to something that makes the land valuable."

"Which makes you suspect . . . ?"

"Whoever actually uncovered the documents. Mrs. Quidley said they were given to her by another historical society member."

"Who?"

"Mr. Ashworth. He's been with the society for years."

"So everything points to him." I snapped my fingers. "Do you think he could have hired the high schoolers to trash the club?"

Ashley frowned. "He would have had to keep a lot of people quiet. My guess is he put Maddox up to it."

I told her what I'd seen in Maddox's tennis bag. "Do you think we have enough to go to the police?"

She squinted. "We need more."

After dinner I played flashlight tag with Dylan behind the house. Ashley tried, but her ankle still felt tender. Mom called me in for a phone call.

"Bryce?" a scratchy voice said, like somebody trying to disguise his voice.

"Yeah, who's this?"

"Listen carefully." Wind noise in the background. "If you want to know who's trying to close the country club, come to the back entrance and wait. Alone."

CHAPTER 65

✸ Ashley ✸

No way was I going to let Bryce go alone.

"Who could this be?" I said into the headset as we rode our ATVs through the field behind our house.

"Caller ID showed a number I didn't recognize—992-something."

"And the voice?"

"Deep. Like a guy."

There were no cars in the parking lot, and the club was dark. The only lights were the lamps above the street and a couple of security ones that stay on all night. The whole place looked spooky in the moonlight.

We parked and made sure no one was watching, then split up and headed for the back of the club. We kept our helmets on so we could communicate in whispers.

"Watch your ankle," Bryce said. "Don't want to have to forfeit our matches."

"Thanks for caring so much."

The closer Bryce got to the club, the less I liked the situation. "What if one of those high schoolers is waiting to pulverize you?"

"Just stay in the shadows," he said. "I have to look alone."

"Sounds like they're on *your* trail, not mine."

I heard something and froze. Bryce stopped too. I got that feeling in the pit of my stomach when you know you've made a bad decision, but there's not much you can do about it. If we turned around and went home we'd spend the next few days wondering what we'd have found out if we'd stayed. And who knew if we could get away anyway?

"What if it's Maddox and his dad?" I whispered.

"What if it's the ghost of Bascom?"

I rolled my eyes, then saw something to our left. A red fox stopped when he spotted us. Then, like he owned the place, he sniffed the wind and kept moving.

I moved from tree to tree, slowly making my way down the hill about 30 yards behind Bryce toward the back entrance. Iron chairs and tables sat outside on the patio. I waited at the edge of the trees while he looked around a bit, then sat.

"You sure this is where he said to come?" I said.

I could barely make out Bryce nodding in the darkness.

A siren wailed in the distance and echoed on the hill behind us. The tennis-court fence loomed like a jagged cloud.

Bryce whispered, "I think somebody's inside." He stood and tiptoed to the window. "Movement in the restaurant. A flashlight? Shadows and light along the back wall."

My heart sank. From where I stood I could see the whole building.

"Bryce, it's a fire!"

CHAPTER 66

☺ *Bryce* ☺

I pulled out my cell phone and punched 911. I could barely hear the operator because a siren was so close. She said they'd already received a call about the fire.

"Who from?" I said.

"I can't give out that information."

Someone ran from the back of the tennis complex, heading for the road.

"Ashley! Come and flag down the firemen and show them where the fire is. I'll catch that guy!"

The spinning lights of the fire engine cast eerie colors on the trees. I was almost to my ATV when someone shouted over a loudspeaker, "Hold it right there!"

A police car screeched to within inches of me. My worst nightmare. Again.

An officer ran toward me. Firemen charged down the hill with axes and hoses. When the officer recognized me, he shook his head.

"The person who started the fire is running that way," I said, pointing.

"Yeah, right."

CHAPTER 67

✽ Ashley ✽

The police called our house, and Sam showed up a few minutes later, his hands deep in his pockets. Then the club manager got there, and I wasn't sure which made him more upset—the fire in the restaurant or us in the parking lot.

"We were able to contain it to the kitchen," the fire chief told the manager. "There's a lot of damage, so you'll have to close until that's repaired."

The manager looked at us and sneered, "Great. Just what we need." He stepped away and made a phone call.

"He should have been glad we called 911," I muttered.

The police officer found out the first call about the fire had been made from the pay phone in front of the club.

Bryce said, "The number didn't happen to start with 992, did it?"

The cop checked his notepad. "Matter of fact, it did."

"That's the number that showed up on our caller ID."

"That should be easy to verify," the officer said, writing everything Bryce said.

Bryce repeated the message he'd heard and said we were trying to get to the bottom of the mystery.

Bryce and I sat in Sam's truck and watched the press pull up, as well as people who worked at the club. We noticed Mr. Grassel but didn't have the heart to talk to him.

Sam's growly voice broke the silence. "Why do you think you two keep running into trouble like this?"

"Just lucky, I guess," I said.

The officer came over, and I rolled down the window. He looked at his notepad, then straight at Bryce. "Lady over here says she heard you mention a fire today," the officer said. "In the kitchen, no less."

Bryce looked like he couldn't believe it. Then another look came over him, like someone had dug a pit and put a sharp stake at the bottom and he was falling in.

"I said that to Miss Davidson and her secretary—Delores. I . . . I j-j-just—"

It was the first time I'd heard Bryce stutter in weeks.

Sam put a hand on his shoulder, and Bryce took a deep breath. "I just said that whoever was trying to shut them down had done everything but start a fire in the kitchen. . . ."

"And it was just a coincidence, eh?" the officer said.

Bryce had a far-off look.

The cop sighed. "No sign of forced entry," he said before moving back to the manager.

"Bet this is the last straw for the club," Sam said. He got out and walked toward the officer.

"What are you thinking, Bryce?" I said.

"Whoever started the fire had to have keys to the club."

"Maybe he hid in there before they closed."

"And whoever ran off went in the direction of Maddox's house."

"But—"

Bryce turned to me. "How could Mr. Ashworth make his son frame me? And how could he know I'd said something about a fire? Doesn't add up."

I felt a twinge in my ankle. "Maybe those old documents don't have a thing to do with this. Could Sean and those other high school guys have heard you?"

Bryce shook his head. "They were outside when I was talking to Miss Davidson."

"Then let's go to Maddox's house and see where he was tonight."

"That'd be real subtle. 'Hey, Maddox, did you call me up and set a fire to frame me?'"

"No, seriously. Maybe we're closer to solving this than we think."

Bryce stared at me, his jaw set. "I'm not backing down until we figure it out."

CHAPTER 68

☺ *Bryce* ☺

That night I tossed and turned like a trapped alligator.
I opened all the windows and even had to get a fan from downstairs.

When I finally did sleep, I dreamed about a fire in some old building, and Ashley, Dylan, and Leigh were trapped. I woke in a sweat with the sheet wrapped around me so tight I could hardly breathe.

Though sunlight was barely peeking over the horizon, I dressed and went to the kitchen. Sam sat there with the morning paper and flipped me the local section.

A story called "Suspicious Blaze Damages Country Club" showed firemen silhouetted against flames and smoke. It didn't say much beyond that two juveniles were questioned and released.

I hate being called a "juvenile," but it sure beat having my name printed.

One of the lead stories on the front page quoted an unnamed source inside the U.S. government who said that they had hard evidence the crash of my dad's flight was no accident but had been caused by a terrorist.

Sam smirked. "'Bout time they got it right."

FedEx delivered Sam a package from Washington, D.C., just before he drove us to tennis camp.

We arrived early, so Ashley and I headed for the courts. Guy zoomed up in his old car. It sounded like the thing could use a new muffler along with everything else. He pulled into the parking lot near a stranger who stood with his arms crossed. Ashley and I edged closer.

"Had it checked out by another buyer last week," Guy said. "It's running really well."

"Brakes sounded rough when you pulled up," the stranger said, opening the hood.

"I'd knock off a hundred for the brakes."

I wanted to hold up a Buyer Beware sign.

They talked about the engine, but it didn't sound like Guy knew much. He said he had changed the oil every 3,000 miles. A likely story.

The stranger opened the trunk and complained about powder all over the floor.

"Right," Guy said. "I had to haul fertilizer and haven't cleaned it out. A shop vac will do the trick."

The guy took it for a test-drive, but Ashley and I didn't stick around to see if Guy made the sale.

"Didn't Guy say he had an apartment when he talked with Leigh?" Ashley said. "Do people in apartments tend their own lawns?"

CHAPTER 69

❧ Ashley ❧

We couldn't count anybody out, the pro-shop cashier included, but I wanted more information about Guy. Was the fertilizer in Guy's trunk really grass killer and thus the clue we were looking for? If so, why was it in his old car and not the new one?

Bryce looked at some shirts in the pro shop while I stood in line at the counter. I grabbed a Snickers bar and shoved it toward the cash register.

As the man returned I said, "Do you know where Guy worked before he came here?"

The man smiled and cocked his head, as if he knew why I was interested. "Don't you think he's a little old for you?"

I faked a laugh. "Can't a girl dream?"

The man leaned forward. "I heard he worked at some big country club in Arizona." He told me the club name and where it was located. "He ran the whole program there. They crowed about him like he was the second coming of Bjorn Borg."

Bjorn Borg? Who's she?

"Is he doing a good job with the tennis camp?" he said.

"Oh, he's great," I said. "Who does the hiring around here?"

A few golfers walked in, and the man grew antsy fast. "Personnel matters are handled in the office."

CHAPTER 70

☺ *Bryce* ☺

Ashley tried to get through our drills, but she was slow and careful. The worst was running suicides. She had to quit before she finished the first one. I thought Guy would call her lazy, but he just had her sit.

The high school guys seemed interested in my running the suicides full tilt. They had learned my last name and used it often.

"Come on, Timberline, move it!"

"Get with the program, Timberline!"

We got a five-minute break to get our lungs going, and Maddox came up to me rubbing his face with a towel. "What did you do to those guys?"

I shook my head. "Must be my shirt. Stripes drive some people crazy."

He smiled. "Funny."

"It's a big misunderstanding," I said. "They think I have it in for a friend of theirs."

Maddox unzipped his tennis bag and pulled out the plastic tube I had seen before. Only this time it was full. To my horror, Maddox opened the tube and sprinkled some on his hands. He offered me some.

"What *is* that stuff?"

"Supposed to keep your hands dry," Maddox said. "Works pretty good."

I shook my head. "Hey, where were you last night?"

"At a movie with Tiffany. Why?"

"Just wondering."

CHAPTER 71

❋ Ashley ❋

By the time we got home, my ankle was sore and swollen again. I iced it and propped it up on the coffee table while Bryce sat at the computer. He said he was trying to get all possible suspects on-screen.

"I'd be happy if Maddox wasn't involved," I said, "but even if that stuff in his bag wasn't the chemical they found in the pool, it doesn't mean he's innocent. He admitted he was up there."

"That's one reason I think he's not guilty," Bryce said. "If he put the stuff in the pool, why would he tell me he was there? He's got to be smarter than that."

I told Bryce to look up the country club where Guy used to work. Bryce keyed in the information, but the search engine asked if he had misspelled it. He tried several different ways, but there wasn't a site for a country club in that town.

Bryce scrolled down, clicked the next page, and scrolled some more. On the ninth page he said, "Aha!" An article popped up from a newspaper in Arizona that had the country club in the headline.

"What's it say?" I said.

He held up a hand. He wrote something down, clicked on another Web site, and typed something in. I was about to throw my ice pack at him when he picked up the phone and started dialing.

"What?"

"The country club where Guy worked went out of business."

CHAPTER 72

☺ *Bryce* ☺

I got the name of the man who had been the owner of the Arizona country club from the article.

When he answered the phone I told him I was calling from Colorado for information about a former employee of his.

"Okay," the man said warily. His voice was shaky, and he sounded old.

"Tennis coach. Good player. Name is Guy Fornay."

Silence. Then, "I don't remember everybody at the club. It's been such a long time. . . ."

"This guy would have run the program. Top dog."

"Our main tennis guy was Ken Bias. I don't recall us ever employing—" He turned from the phone and said, "Honey, you remember anybody named Guy Fornay?"

His wife said something, and then he came back on. "I'm sorry. Neither one of us remembers anybody with that name."

I described Guy, and the man said he couldn't remember anyone who looked like that working at his club.

"How long ago did you close?"

"It'll be six years this Christmas."

CHAPTER 73

✖ Ashley ✖

Since Guy's résumé had to be fake, we figured he might be in tight with Mr. Ashworth, who had put him up to the vandalism. Maybe the high school guys had helped him. Before we went to the police, we had to make sure.

"We have to get him on his turf," Bryce said, punching in Guy's name for all of Colorado. Nothing came back.

"What about the name on the car title?" I said.

"We tried Castle Rock, but it didn't show anything." He punched it in for the whole state and got a newspaper article from Crested Butte. A Wesley Collins had been arrested for breaking and entering at a movie star's house. The article didn't include a picture but said he was 24 years old.

Bryce snapped his fingers and ran upstairs. He came back with a crumpled piece of paper. "Look what I found in Leigh's wastebasket."

He logged on to a reverse phone directory and typed in the number Guy had advertised to call about his car for sale.

The service confirmed it was a Red Rock number, but no other specific information was available.

"So we know he has an apartment in Red Rock," I said. "How do we find out where it is?"

Bryce looked at his watch. "We follow him home."

"On our ATVs? On the highway?"

"No. I've got a better idea."

"You sure he's still at the country club?"

"He usually stays till six. It's worth a try."

CHAPTER 74

☻ *Bryce* ☻

Strapping the telescope on my ATV wasn't easy, but soon
we were off. Ashley brought sandwiches in case we didn't get back
in time for dinner.

As we drove past the country club I slowed and checked which
car Guy would be driving. If he had sold the old one, the Corvette
would be here. But it was the clunker. Ashley and I rode into a cul-
de-sac a hundred yards away. Construction guys were pouring ce-
ment at a new house, so we parked at the back of the site, where the
ATVs wouldn't be in the way.

I lugged the telescope up the hill. After 20 minutes of climbing we reached the top of the ridge. A clearing looked down on the outdoor courts and gave us a perfect view of town. In fact, a perfect view of just about everything.

"From here we can see the main road. As long as he goes from here to his apartment, we have him."

"What if he gets on I-25? He could go anywhere."

"At six he's going to be hungry. I'm hoping he'll go home for something to eat."

We could see the door of the indoor courts, and Ashley watched as I focused the telescope. Problem was, we couldn't see the parking lot, so we had to make sure we caught him walking out.

Talking about him being hungry made me hungry, so we broke out the sandwiches. There's something about watching someone you think is a criminal that makes you feel more alive and hungry.

I was in the middle of a ham and cheese when Ashley said, "What if he goes through the club to the parking lot?"

A hunk of ham caught in my throat, and I thought I was going to die. I took a drink. "That's a problem."

Ashley looked at her watch. "I'd better climb down to the parking lot. We'll use the headphones."

"Will they reach that far?"

"One way to find out."

At 5:55 I heard the Ashleymobile fire up. She came to a stop a few seconds later, and the engine died. I kept an eye on the side door of the tennis center and another on the scope, watching for the best place to pick up Guy's car on the main road.

"Can you hear me?" Ashley said.

I waited a second just to scare her. Yeah, I know. I'm sick.

"Bryce?"

"I hear you."

"Creep."

"Sorry."

I spotted a white car on the main road behind me and timed it from the point it passed the country club to the spot where the trees broke along the main road. Two minutes, 13 seconds.

"Okay, Guy's coming out of the club."

I clicked the Start button on my stopwatch and focused the telescope. The last thing I wanted was to sneeze and lose him.

At one minute and 44 seconds, Guy's car came into view. He motored down the hill toward town, and I was surprised he could get the old beater up to that speed.

I watched him wait at a traffic light, then turn right over the I-25 bridge. I held my breath. If he got in the left lane it meant he was going south on the interstate. He kept right.

"What's going on?" Ashley said.

"Here's where it gets tricky. If he goes behind a building, I could lose him. Nope, he's headed for the main road, past RadioShack . . . now Safeway. Okay, he's going into the shopping center." He went behind a laundry, and I kept the telescope moving at what I thought was his rate of speed. When I saw him come out the other side, I gave a huge sigh.

"Where is he now?" Ashley said.

"Good news and bad news. We still don't know where he lives, but we do know he likes Taco Bell."

CHAPTER 75

✖ Ashley ✖

I raced back up the hill, and Bryce turned the scope over to me. I watched Guy sit in the restaurant and eat his burrito, then pull out an envelope and study it.

"I suppose it's too much to ask of this telescope to be able to read that."

Bryce frowned. "It's maxed out. At this distance, the document would have to be on a tripod too."

Guy left his trash on the table—the slob—and walked to his car. He tossed the note in the backseat, and I followed him carefully to the main road. He turned back the way he had come and pulled into the grocery-store lot, then Blockbuster.

Bryce perked up. "If he's going for a movie, maybe he'll go home and watch it."

"You think he borrowed the ATV and did all the vandalism?"

Bryce shrugged. "He's as likely as anyone."

"How are we going to confront him?" I said. "Call him up and say we know he likes Taco Bell?"

"Maybe we can trick him into confessing."

"Guy doesn't seem the tricking type."

A few minutes later he went across the parking lot to the back of another fast-food place.

"He's getting out," I said. "Opening the trunk. Dumping stuff in a trash bin—yeah, shaking a bag out like crazy. Looks like fertilizer. Opening his back door and tossing . . . he must have a ton of hamburger and taco wrappers back there. He's dumping everything. What kind of a selfish jerk uses someone else's Dumpster?"

"You think he threw the note out too?" Bryce said.

Guy finally pulled out and headed for town. Several times I thought we'd lost him, but he finally came out near an elementary school at a small apartment building called the Allerton. We watched which entrance he went in, then grabbed the telescope and headed down.

CHAPTER 76

☻ *Bryce* ☻

It was eight o'clock and still light out when we parked our ATVs and walked to the Dumpster. The smell made me wish I hadn't eaten.

I lifted the green lid, and a thousand flies flew out, along with a few bees. Ashley's look told me she wasn't going near the thing, and I wondered myself if it was worth it.

Most of the trash was in clear plastic bags. But on top were empty tennis-ball cans, food wrappers, Starbucks coffee cups, newspapers still rolled up with rubber bands, and CDs that looked like they had warped in the sun.

I didn't see an envelope, but there was no way to be sure other than to lean over the side and dig in. I took a deep breath and started moving things around. I threw the tennis-ball cans and newspapers to the back, revealing a layer of stuff I hadn't seen. An empty bag of weed killer, a box cutter with the razor blade sticking out, old grocery store and Blockbuster receipts, and at the bottom of the pile a white envelope, stained with coffee—at least I hoped it was coffee. I leaned a little farther and almost had it when the side of the Dumpster pressing against my lungs made me tip back and hit the ground, gasping.

"Anything?" Ashley said.

Before I could answer, a car screeched to a stop. "Dumpster dining, Timberline?"

It was Adam's Apple and three other guys. Sean poked his head out the back window. "This is what I call luck!" he said, getting out.

"Let's get out of here," Ashley whispered, teeth clenched.

"Hang on," I said. I took a deep breath, leaned into the garbage, and grabbed the envelope. I stuffed the soggy thing in my pocket and yelled at Ashley to run.

We took off across the parking lot, through a grassy area, and across an interstate access road. A car door slammed behind us, and tires squealed.

Ashley stayed right with me, her ankle as good as before she twisted it. The car kicked up dust behind us, so we cut across another grassy area to a gas station/truck stop. We ran inside, hoping the guys wouldn't see us.

When they pulled up I thought about hiding in the bathrooms, but Ashley grabbed my hand and we ran out the other side, ducking behind several drop boxes for FedEx, UPS, and regular mail.

The car rumbled around the parking lot, went past us, then around again. The guys hollered, "Where'd they go?" and "I saw them go in there!"

When we were sure they were gone, Ashley and I ran toward the Allerton.

CHAPTER 77

✖ Ashley ✖

We stopped when we got to the elementary school across from the apartments. We went to the empty playground, and I made sure I sat upwind of Bryce, who smelled like the garbage bin. We caught our breath, studying the apartment building.

Bryce pulled the note from his pocket and handed it to me. "You do the honors. Let's hope I didn't go through all that for some love note."

The envelope had *Guy* written on the front. I pulled out a plain piece of white paper folded twice. The note looked like it had been printed by a laser printer.

Announcement is coming Saturday. That's when you get
yours in small bills, as requested, in your box. Then leave
and don't come back.

Now *this* was evidence. Bryce was looking over my shoulder. If
he hadn't smelled so bad, I'd have hugged him.

☾ *Bryce* ☾

After I'd showered, Ashley and I compared notes. We both felt Guy was the vandal but that he was working with someone, probably Mr. Ashworth.

"The key is to catch whoever puts the payment in Guy's box," she said.

My mind spun. If we played this right, we'd solve our biggest mystery, but if something went wrong, Guy and whoever was working with him could get away. "I have to get into that mail room tomorrow and figure out how to get this done."

Someone knocked, and we opened the door to Sam. "I have something you may want to see," he said. "Your decision."

"About Dad's plane?"

He nodded. "It's the reason Washington knows the crash wasn't an accident."

CHAPTER 79

❀ Ashley ❀

Fear swept over me, but Bryce and I both said we wanted to see whatever Sam had to show us, and Leigh came along too. We found Mom in the living room, which has the biggest TV, and Sam put in a DVD. A bunch of warnings flashed on the screen. Top secret and all that.

We had found out a few months before about Sam's secret past. It's a long story and complicated, but it made us appreciate him more, not hate him, which is what he was afraid it would do.

Two masked guys with big guns stood against a wall. Even after seeing this type of thing on the news, it gave me the willies. The two were out of focus, but you could tell they weren't there to give you a warm, cuddly feeling.

Somebody yelled something in another language, and a guy wearing a dark hood with cutouts for his mouth and eyes stepped in front of the camera.

He said a couple of sentences in his own language, and then he spoke in pretty good English. "I am Asim bin Asawe, and this message is to the American imperialists who want to overthrow our way of life. We killed the murderer of our children, the one, along with others, who gunned down our comrades-in-arms. We took down his plane. It was not an accident as your lying media has said. It was an act of holy vengeance, and more will follow."

The DVD cut to a grainy clip of a rocket being launched from a boat. The smoke and flame lit up the sky. Sam stopped the DVD.

"He's talking about you, Sam," Bryce said. "He still thinks he killed you in that crash."

"That's the face of evil," Mom said. "Killing all those innocent men, women, and children, and calling it a holy act . . ."

I'd had nightmares about this guy. I pictured him tall and snarling like a wolf, spitting when he talked. I thought he would be ugly, battle-scarred, the kind of guy who runs over people with a tank and doesn't think twice.

But when he stepped in front of the camera I could tell he was standing on something to make him look taller.

What a wimp. Hides behind a mask. Kills people from a distance. He's nothing but a coward trying to scare us.

Leigh shook her head and turned away. Sam sat on the couch and put an arm around her. "I'd like to be able to shield you from this type of thing, but I think it's better you know. We'll get him one day. And the other terrorists who want to control our lives."

I know the Bible says that the love God gives you pushes out fear. I don't think that means you're never afraid of anything, but if you do stuff just because you're afraid, it's not from God. God loves us so much that we don't have to be afraid of idiots like this.

I decided not to be afraid of that kook or anybody else doing bad stuff.

Including the vandals at the country club.

CHAPTER 80

☺ *Bryce* ☺

I called Jill Davidson's office the next morning and left a
message asking if I could meet with her during our lunch break. I
didn't get a call back but went to the office by myself. Delores sat at
her desk with a headset on. She held up a finger as I walked in.

"Yes, we can mail your refund early next week," she said. She
had a pained look, and I wondered if she knew about the announcement coming Saturday. "Yes, ma'am, we've gotten a lot of calls. I'm
sorry you had a bad experience and I understand."

As she talked, I walked past the mailboxes. Each had a person's
name under it. There was room for small packages and envelopes,

but not much more. I wondered how much Guy was supposed to be paid and whether it would fit.

If we could believe the note, the money would be put into Guy's mailbox Saturday. If we could somehow be there, we could catch Guy and his contact person. I moved down the hall and peeked in Jill's office. It was empty and the light was off, but I noticed a small black box on her desk. I'd seen one before, but I couldn't remember where.

"Jill said you might stop by," Delores called to me. "What was it you needed?"

I had to make up something fast. "The historical documents," I blurted out. "My sister and I heard about them. I'm interested in the Bascom guy. Thought I might do a paper on him after school starts." I actually had thought about that, by the way.

Delores smiled. "Well, aren't you a studious one? I wish my son was that interested in school."

She went on about her son, and I tried to act interested.

"When I found the documents," she said, "I didn't know how important they'd be."

"*You* found them?"

She nodded. "We got a new safe, so I had to take everything out of the old one."

"What did you do with them?"

She furrowed her brow. "Jill and the manager and I agreed they were worthless, but I called the historical society, and Mr. Ashworth picked them up."

"Did you notice any pages with numbers? One was a picture of the house, but we think there were others."

"I remember the house but no numbers," she said as she wheeled behind her desk and opened a file cabinet. "But I made photocopies before we turned them over."

"You did?" I said. I wanted to hug Delores. "Can I see them?"

She pulled out a folder and plopped it on her desk. "If it will make your report better."

In the middle of the pile I found the page Ashley had described. It was clearly a drawing of the old house, but the pages before it were just letters. The copy machine had numbered the pages, but 18 and 19 were missing.

When I asked her about them Delores shook her head and took the stack back. "Those should be here." She riffled through the stack, then went through it again.

She looked closely at the house drawing. "This was rolled up and tied with a shoelace that looked about a hundred years old. I tried to tie it back the way I found it, but I don't know if it held—it was almost dust."

"What was on those pages?"

"Well, one looked kind of like a will with a bunch of *wherefores* and *herewiths* all over the place."

"And the other one?"

Delores looked at me like I was asking too many questions so I flashed her my I'm-just-a-poor-little-middle-school-student smile.

She closed the folder and didn't say more.

CHAPTER 81

✖ Ashley ✖

When Saturday morning rolled around, Bryce and I were ready. Guy had seemed giddy toward the end of the week and stopped making us run suicides. For the first time in two weeks he actually seemed happy, and Bryce and I knew why.

We kept our distance from the high schoolers. Bryce and I saw them whispering and laughing, probably about what Sean was going to do to Bryce.

The singles final was played at nine with the doubles to follow. Bryce and I made our preparations to catch the crook after we heard the manager of the club was going to make a special announcement following the doubles final.

By 10:15 the singles match was over, and we took the court, volleying with Maddox and Tiffany. Mr. Ashworth was in the stands. My stomach was already in knots, and the finals caused it to gurgle.

It's weird playing in front of people—even if it's only a few dozen. I'm used to people waiting and watching idly, but when they're really following the game it makes you nervous.

Wouldn't my dad have gotten a kick out of seeing us in the championship? Mom and Sam sat on the grass near the hill and smiled.

Guy climbed into the umpire chair at the side of the court. We didn't have line judges or ball boys/girls, but Guy was king of the court, at least for one more match.

Maddox won the toss and the first four points easily. We switched sides and Bryce won his serve—not as easily, but he won. Tiffany had a double fault but got most of her first serves in. Maddox jumped on one of my returns, and Tiffany held serve. Then it was my turn, trailing 1–2.

I can usually get the jitters out of my system after a few games, but serving is different. Tossing the ball, hitting it in the box on the other side—it all looks easy on TV, but when your hands are shaking and you're thinking about who might have hired Guy to close the club while you're trying to hit to Maddox's backhand, it can be nerve-racking.

CHAPTER 82

☻ *Bryce* ☻

Ashley's serve bounced into the net. I whispered to her to settle down. If we lost this game we'd be down 3–1.

"Pull it together," I said. "What's wrong?"

"What if Guy gets away with the money and we never find out who hired him?"

I smiled at her. "Have we ever not figured out a mystery? We're going to be okay. Take a breath and enjoy this. Let's show old Maddox a thing or two about tennis."

She played better, but we lost the game. Everyone held serve after that, and the first set went to them, 6–3.

We got a couple of minutes to get a drink and rest. It was 11:00, and the sun was right over us. My shirt was soaked and my hair dripping.

I rubbed a towel over my head and looked into the crowd. A bunch of campers yelled for Maddox and Tiffany. Hayley cheered for us. I looked for Duncan, but I think he couldn't stand watching something he wasn't part of.

Then I spotted Mr. Ashworth moving toward the country club. I jabbed Ashley's shoulder and nodded at him. She raised her eyebrows. "Won't be long until we find out the truth."

"I hope it will take two more sets."

CHAPTER 83

❋ Ashley ❋

Bryce had the first serve in the second set, and he meant business. The ball zinged by my ear and landed just inside the line. Tiffany ran, but Bryce put so much spin on it that it hit the fence, out of reach.

"That was out!" Maddox yelled.

A murmur rose from the crowd.

"Second service," Guy said.

"What?" Bryce said.

"The ball was out. Second service."

I couldn't believe it. "You've got to be kidding me. It was on this side of the line."

Was this about more than Bryce's first serve? Did Guy know we were on to him?

Bryce shook his head, and I knew he wanted to argue, but we both knew it wouldn't do any good.

"Let's show them how to play doubles," I said, teeth clenched.

Bryce didn't lose a point the rest of the game. Tiffany must have felt our intensity because she served like a scared mouse and lost. Then it was my turn.

Suddenly I forgot about the investigation, Dad's plane, Leigh's car search, the funny thing Dylan had said to me that morning, lunch, and all the other things that had been running through my mind. I focused on one thing—the little yellow-green ball. Before I knew it, the game was over, and they had gotten only one point.

Maddox held serve and so did Tiffany, but we had turned things around and won, 6–3.

Third and deciding set coming up.

CHAPTER 84

☺ *Bryce* ☺

When Mr. Ashworth returned to his seat he'd had more than enough time to put something in Guy's box. The club manager stood nearby, along with Jill, Delores, and Mr. Grassel. Everyone had turned out for our finale.

Mr. Ashworth yelled at Maddox as we gulped Gatorade. Sam shook his head. Mom seemed aghast that anyone would treat their kid that way.

Tiffany served first in the third set, and it was important for us to get off to a good start. We made a couple of dumb mistakes, and she got all her first serves in, which really put the pressure on. We were down 1–0.

Ashley fought hard and held her serve. Then Maddox did the same. Two games later it was 3–2, their favor, with Ashley serving when it happened. Ashley hit to Tiffany's backhand, and I hit a volley at Maddox's feet. His reflexes were lightning, and he managed to short hop it and lob the ball over my head. I ran to the baseline as Ashley hit the ball to Tiffany, now at the net. She dinked the ball off the top of her racket, just over the net, and Ashley raced in for it. It was the worst shot in the history of tennis, but it worked like a drop shot. Just as the ball was about to hit the ground the second time, Ashley lunged and I heard her yelp. She went down and grabbed her ankle.

Guy climbed down from his chair and hovered over Ashley like a doctor. She stood and limped, then sat on the bench at the side of the court. Maddox and Tiffany kept their distance. I guess they were hoping we'd have to forfeit.

I leaned down. "What's the word, Ash?"

"I'm not sure I can walk, let alone play."

"It's okay. We can stop."

She looked over at Mom and Sam. Some high school guys sat behind them, one of them Adam's Apple. Ashley grabbed her racket and hobbled back onto the court as the crowd clapped.

We lost her serve and were down 5–2 after Maddox served. Ashley moved like an old woman, so I knew I had to pick up the slack.

We held my serve, then broke Tiffany's. When Ashley won the last point of her serve, it was 5–5. Maddox held serve, and so did I.

6–6.

"We will play a nine-point tiebreaker," Guy said from the chair. "First team to five points wins the match."

CHAPTER 85

✖ Ashley ✖

The nerves switched from us to people in the stands. They clapped and cheered. Hayley put both hands to her mouth and shook with excitement. A tennis tiebreaker is like overtime in football or basketball. And a nine-point tiebreaker is the best because you don't keep playing on and on until someone wins by two. Whoever gets to five first wins.

I wasn't nervous anymore. The pain in my ankle took that away. Some people think girls aren't as competitive as boys, and I'll admit Bryce seems to have competition flowing through his veins. But girls can be just as competitive. I know I am. I wanted to win.

I returned Tiffany's serve deep in her court, and she managed to get back only a weak lob, which Bryce put away. I served into the net the first serve, my second tipping the top of the net and hopping out-of-bounds. Double fault. It was 1–1.

The crowd groaned, and Bryce banged his racket against his hand. "That's okay. Come on—four more points."

I got my next serve in and Bryce faked to his left, then changed direction and picked off a volley from Maddox and put it past Tiffany. 2–1, our favor.

To my surprise, instead of a screaming fastball, Maddox served up a pork chop that I swatted straight at Tiffany. She was so surprised by it that she stuck up her racket and missed. 3–1, us. I figured we were in good shape, but when Maddox hit his second serve to my backhand, I managed to only dribble it to our net.

3–2, our favor.

We switched courts. We needed only two more points to win. They needed three.

It was Bryce's serve, and he sidled up to me as we walked past the benches. "What do you say we try the dipsy do?"

I chuckled. "Might work."

I studied Tiffany's eyes, and just as Bryce was about to toss the ball I took three steps to my right, which blocked Tiffany's view. Instead of hitting an overhead serve, Bryce let the ball fall and plinked an underhand drop shot with lots of spin just over my right shoulder. It's a risky move, but we had practiced this a hundred times.

Tiffany reacted well and ran in. But I moved up and as soon as she got the ball over the net, I smacked it into the open court for a winner. It was something the Harlem Globetrotters would have done if they played tennis.

Some people booed. Maddox swung his racket and scraped the top of it against the court.

"Pay attention out there!" his father yelled.

4–2. *One more point!*

I figured we had the match. Steam was nearly coming out of Maddox's ears. Bryce hit a blistering serve that I thought would be an ace until Maddox hit it twice as hard two inches past my head. I turned and watched it just catch the line on our side. Bryce and I looked at Guy, who extended both arms, palms down. In.

"Four to three, Timberlines. Tiffany, you'll serve for the match."

When Tiffany served it was Maddox's turn to be a Globetrotter. He raced almost to the middle of the court, then just as I hit it to the open court, he raced back and put away my shot.

His dad threw his fist in the air. "Yeah!"

Bryce raised his eyebrows and shrugged.

"Four to four," Guy shouted, rubbing his hands.

CHAPTER 86

☺ *Bryce* ☺

I bounced on my toes, trying to stay loose. Hot as it was, that wasn't hard. I'd begun to feel a cramp in my left leg. I glanced at the sidelines as Tiffany moved to the baseline. Trophies lined a table with the two big ones for the champs of the singles and doubles. I didn't want the wimpy trophy this time.

Tiffany tossed the ball and got her first serve in. I hit it back, making sure I got it past Maddox. It hit close to the baseline, and Tiffany backed up and hit a forehand over Ashley's head. I moved left, keeping an eye on Maddox. He stayed in position, but I hit a high backhand I was sure he couldn't get to. When Tiffany backed up, I saw my chance and raced to the net.

Ashley and I stood like soldiers waiting for an incoming attack. Maddox retreated as Tiffany swung and hit a sky-high lob that didn't look like it would reach the net. My heart pounded, knowing this was our chance for the championship.

The crowd sat silent. Everything went in slow motion as the ball arced toward me. Instead of taking it in the air, I moved a step back to let it bounce. "I got it," I said. I wanted to hit this ball to Wyoming.

But instead of hitting the court and bouncing high, the ball glanced off the top of the net and plopped onto our side. I had only one chance to get it, and that was to dive. I got my racket under the ball before it touched down and flicked it just over the net where it bounced twice before Maddox could get to it.

But my racket hit the net.

People screamed and clapped. Guy climbed down. Maddox patted Tiffany's back as she hung her head.

I turned to Ashley. "My racket hit the net."

"You sure?" she said. "I didn't see it."

"I felt it."

Guy shook hands with Tiffany and Maddox, then turned to us.

"My racket hit the net on that last point," I said.

Guy raised his eyebrows. "I didn't see it."

"But it did. That means you guys win. Good shot, Tiffany. You deserve it."

Tiffany looked like she had won a gold medal in the Olympics. Maddox gave her a high five, then shook our hands.

Maddox's dad whooped and hollered. I figured he wouldn't be there when the police arrived.

Everyone else stood around, stunned, like they had just seen a car accident. I stuffed my racket in my tennis bag and pulled out my cell phone to dial the police.

"I was proud when I thought you two had won that match," Sam said. I buried my head in his chest, and he patted my sweaty back. He leaned close so only I could hear. "But I'm even prouder now."

CHAPTER 87

✖ Ashley ✖

My ankle felt worse, probably because we lost, but there were lots of people who came up and congratulated us. Hayley stuck around the longest, apologizing for the way she'd treated me. She couldn't believe Duncan hadn't watched the finals. "And my parents will be so upset they suspected you. They'll probably say you can sleep over for a whole month."

The club manager called everyone to order and handed out the trophies. Everybody clapped for Bryce and me, but they saved their biggest ovation for Maddox and Tiffany.

The manager asked people to sit. "We have a rather sad announcement to end our tournament. A mailing went out today concerning the closing of the country club."

A few gasped, but most knew this was coming. Bryce jogged up the hill where a police car pulled in.

"So we want to thank you all for participating in what will be our final event of the club." He glanced at the police car and stammered.

I raised my hand. "You might want to hold off on the announcement a moment."

Bryce led the officer down the hill. He couldn't help smiling, and I couldn't help watching Guy squirm.

"Mr. Fornay?" the officer said.

"What's going on?" Guy said.

"We have information that you're responsible for the vandalism at this country club over the past two weeks," the officer said. "You're under arrest. You have the right to remain silent. Anything you say—"

Guy looked at him like the man had just smashed his racket. "Me? What proof do you have? I deny any involvement in—"

"And we have reason to believe that you've been paid for your crime. Care to explain that?"

Guy's face blanched as white as his tennis outfit. "What makes you think—?"

"We know you spread the grass killer," Bryce said. "And you set me up. The only question now is who put you, Guy—actually Wesley—up to it."

That we knew his real name seemed to send Guy over the edge. "Okay, look—I didn't want to do it, but then I was threatened. I swear, they made me do it."

"Who?" the officer said.

"Whoever is behind this. They hired me and then said if I didn't cooperate, there would be a big lawsuit and the police would get involved . . . and with my past, I couldn't have the police involved."

"Tell us who," the officer said.

"I don't know! It started with a phone call. A man with a weird voice offered me a lot of money to teach tennis. Sent me a made-up résumé. After I got here, notes showed up in my mailbox. I left notes saying I didn't want to do stuff like that, and that's when I got threatened."

The officer looked at Bryce. "You said you have proof of who this is?"

Bryce nodded and whispered, "Don't let anybody leave. I'll be right back."

CHAPTER 88

☻ *Bryce* ☻

I knew from watching crime shows that I shouldn't touch the money in Guy's mailbox, but I couldn't help looking at the green zippered bag in there and wondering how much was inside.

I grabbed the video camera I had hidden behind a plant on Delores's desk and punched the recorder off. I hit Rewind and went back outside. Our camera has a fold-out screen you can see from a few feet away.

"Want to tell us what you're doing?" the manager said.

"Sure," I said, looking to make sure Mr. Ashworth was there. "The person who got Guy involved left a note that said he'd be paid as soon as the club's closing was announced. I set this camera up in front of the mailbox and started recording before our doubles match. Guy's box was empty. Now there's a green cash bag in there."

I punched Play and held down the Fast Forward button. People crowded around. In just a few seconds the screen showed the same picture of mailboxes for almost an hour. Then Delores showed up, watered plants, and moved away.

"There's your culprit." Mr. Ashworth chuckled. "This is ridiculous."

"Just hold on," the officer said.

Finally someone holding a green bag moved into the shot. They were making sure no one was watching. Then, slowly, the figure filled the screen. Black pants. White shirt. Short brown hair.

A female.

She stuffed the bag in Guy's box and turned.

Jill Davidson.

CHAPTER 89

❋ Ashley ❋

As soon as the officer cuffed Jill, things clicked. She had been the first one on the scene when Guy nearly ran me over on the first day of camp. She had been watching to see if Guy would do what he was told. She had also found Bryce's key in his ATV and ordered Guy back to the country club for a joyride.

"But how did you make your voice so deep?" Guy said.

When Jill didn't answer, Bryce did. "Simple. Voice changer. I saw one in Jill's office. Finally figured out what it was."

"But why, Jill?" the manager said. "Why would you want to shut down the very business that pays your bills?"

Jill just stared at him.

I stepped forward. "She had access to the historical documents, and there are pages missing. We find those documents, and the mystery will be solved."

The manager stomped off toward the club as the officer put Jill in the squad car.

"I've been set up!" Guy yelled as another officer arrived to take him away.

A few minutes later the manager came out with a bunch of papers he had found in Jill's office. Bryce and I knew what we were looking for and found the pages at the bottom of the stack.

"Last Will and Testament of John Bascom" was printed on the first one. It was Bascom's scrawl, and it took us a while to decipher it. It said Bascom wanted his house (diagram included) to go to his wife and children when he died. In the third paragraph we found what we were looking for.

> On the last page of this will, I include a map to all my
> worldly goods, hidden in a strongbox and buried close to
> the house. I bequeath all the contents therein to my wife
> and children. Should they not be living, I give it to my
> cousin, Jeb Clavendar.

The next page showed a crudely drawn map. The manager pointed to where the house used to sit above the courts. Mr. Ashworth said he had a tape measure in his truck and went to get it. We stepped off 50 yards from an old tree stump and found remnants of a huge rock that had been moved. Then 30 feet due west brought us to the middle of court #2.

The manager held up a pink slip of paper. "Here's a callback for

Jill from a construction contractor. Think it might have anything to do with this?"

Mr. Ashworth knew the contractor and called him. When he hung up, he said, "He got a call from some weird-sounding guy who wanted to know how much it would cost to dig up a tennis court."

Mr. Ashworth turned to Bryce and me. "I misjudged you both. If it wasn't for you, Jill would have gotten out of here without our ever figuring this out."

The manager stuck out his hand. "That goes double for me. If this place ever opens again, you two are lifetime members."

CHAPTER 90

Bryce

Three days later, a construction crew from Mr. Ashworth's company dug up a 20-foot section of court #2.

Ashley and I rode our ATVs, and she stopped at a big yard and pointed. Sean held a long garden hose and spread water back and forth on the brown grass. We couldn't help smiling.

An article in that day's paper quoted an officer who said Jill confessed that she had seen the map and formed a plan. Guy was a friend of a friend from Crested Butte, and she figured he would help if she promised enough money. He had put a down payment on the Corvette with his first payment.

"I'm sad to see that court go," Ashley said. "I ran a lot of suicides there."

Workers chipped away at the surface until they had the concrete loose. Then they brought a backhoe in and started digging. Ashley and I looked on like proud parents at a Sunday school Christmas concert. When the guy on the backhoe stopped and yelled, we moved close.

The men dug with shovels until they reached a box about the size of a large piece of luggage. It had a rusty lock on the front.

Mr. Ashworth cut the lock and opened the box.

"It's just an old dress and a bunch of letters," a grizzled, sunburned man said.

The manager held up the dress.

"I bet this was his daughter's," Ashley said. "The one who died young."

Underneath were stacks and stacks of letters, old newspapers from the 1800s, and a small box of jewelry.

The manager's face fell. He stepped back and pulled out his cell phone. The construction crew moved to their lunch pails and water bottles.

Ashley and I looked into the box. "All that planning to shut down the country club for nothing," she said.

"Yeah, what a waste."

Ashley moved some things at the bottom of the box. "Something's funny down there." She placed her palm on the bottom and measured to the top of the box, then did the same on the outside. "I don't think this is the real bottom."

I leaned in and saw a fabric loop mashed to the side. I grabbed it and pulled. The bottom loosened and came up. We stepped back and let the sun hit the contents. Silver coins lay stacked at one end. Gold nuggets sparkled at the other.

Ashley grinned. "Looks like we *are* lifetime members."

Jerry B. Jenkins (jerryjenkins.com) is the writer of the Left Behind series. He owns the Jerry B. Jenkins Christian Writers Guild, an organization dedicated to mentoring aspiring authors. Former vice president for publishing for the Moody Bible Institute of Chicago, he also served many years as editor of *Moody* magazine and is now Moody's writer-at-large.

His writing has appeared in publications as varied as *Reader's Digest, Parade, Guideposts,* in-flight magazines, and dozens of other periodicals. Jenkins's biographies include books with Billy Graham, Hank Aaron, Bill Gaither, Luis Palau, Walter Payton, Orel Hershiser, and Nolan Ryan, among many others. His books appear regularly on the *New York Times, USA Today, Wall Street Journal,* and *Publishers Weekly* best-seller lists.

Jerry is also the writer of the nationally syndicated sports story comic strip *Gil Thorp,* distributed to newspapers across the United States by Tribune Media Services.

Jerry and his wife, Dianna, live in Colorado and have three grown sons and three grandchildren.

Chris Fabry is a writer and broadcaster who lives in Colorado. He has written more than 40 books, including collaboration on the Left Behind: The Kids series.

You may have heard his voice on Focus on the Family, Moody Broadcasting, or Love Worth Finding. He has also written for Adventures in Odyssey and Radio Theatre.

Chris is a graduate of the W. Page Pitt School of Journalism at Marshall University in Huntington, West Virginia. He and his wife, Andrea, have been married 22 years and have nine children, two birds, two dogs, and one cat.

RED ROCK MYSTERIES

BRYCE AND ASHLEY TIMBERLINE are normal 13-year-old twins, except for one thing—they discover action-packed mystery wherever they go. Wanting to get to the bottom of any mystery, these twins find themselves on a nonstop search for truth.

CP0140

The Wormling

From the minds of Jerry B. Jenkins and Chris Fabry comes a thrilling new action-packed fantasy that pits ultimate evil against ultimate good.

Book I
The Book of the King

Book II
The Sword of the Wormling

Book III
The Changeling

Book IV
The Minions of Time

Book V
The Author's Blood

All 5 books available now!

CP0138